The Future Adventures of
Sienne Vhartan

Tyree Campbell

Sienne Vhartan
by Tyree Campbell

All rights reserved. No part of this book may be reproduced or transmitted in any form or by any means, electronic or mechanical, including photocopying or recording or by any information storage and retrieval systems, without expressed written consent of the author and/or artists.

Sienne Vhartan is a work of fiction. Names, characters, places, and incidents are products of the author's imagination. Any resemblance to actual events or persons, living or dead, is entirely coincidental.

Story copyright owned by Tyree Campbell
Cover illustration "Lagatha" by Richard E. Schell
Cover design by Marcia A. Borell

First Printing, April 2025

Hiraeth Publishing
P.O. Box 1248
Tularosa, NM 88352
e-mail: hiraethsubs@yahoo.com

Visit www.hiraethsffh.com for online science fiction, fantasy, horror, scifaiku, and more. Stop by our online bookstore for novels, magazines, anthologies, and collections. **Support the small, independent press...and your First Amendment rights.**

Also by Tyree Campbell

Nyx Series (Novels):
Nyx: Malache
Nyx: Mystere
Nyx: The Protectors
Nyx: Pangaea
Nyx: The Redoubt

Yoelin Thibbony Rescues (Novels)
The Butterfly and the Sea Dragon *
The Moth and the Flame *
*The Thursday Child**
Avatar
The End of Innocence

Lark Series (Novels)
The Desert Lark
The Iphajean Lark
The Justice Lark
The Traffic Lark
The Illusion Lark

Armed Do-gooder Series (Novels)
Bailey Belvedere
Sienne Vhartan

Novels:
The Adventures of Colo Collins & Tama Toledo in Space and Time
The Adventures of Colo Collins & Tama Toledo in Love and in Trouble
Aoife's Kiss
The Breathless Stars
The Dice of God
The Dog at the Foot of the Bed
The Dog at War

Gallium Girl
Heir Apparent
Indigo
Iuliae: Past Tense
The Quinx Effect
Starwinders: Nohana's Heart
Starwinders: Nohana's Triangles
Thuvia, Maid of Earth
A Wolf to Guard the Door
The Woman from the Institute

Superheroine Novellas:
Bombay Sapphire 1 **
Bombay Sapphire 2 **
Bombay Sapphire 3 **
Bombay Sapphire 4 **
Bombay Sapphire 5
Oliva Sudden 1
Peridot 1
Peridot 2
Peridot 3
Peridot 4
Voyeuse 1
Voyeuse 2
Voyeuse 3

Collections:
AbracaDrabble
Drink Before the War
A Nice Girl Like You
(published by Khimairal, Inc)
Quantum Women *

Religious Fiction
Miracle at the Foundry
At the Hour of Our Death

Novellas:
Becoming Jade
Cloudburst
Future Tense
The Girl on the Dump
The Martian Women
Sabit the Sumerian
Sarrow

Poetry Collections
A Danger to Self and Others

SF for Younger Readers
Pyra and the Tektites 1
Pyra (graphic novel) 1
Pyra and the Tektites 2
Pyra (graphic novel) 2
Pyra and the Tektites 3
Pyra and the Tektites 4
Pyra and the Tektites 5
Pyra and the Tektites 6

* published by Nomadic Delirium Press

** published by Pro Se Press

All titles are available from the Shop at
www.hiraethsffh.com

For my readers: I won't stop if you don't…

001: Close Encounter

The woman was standing on the shoulder of the road looking like she might or might not want a ride. Attired as she was in a lemon-yellow shift that reached to just above her knees, and standing slightly hipshot, her right leg out and bent at the knee, she might have been hitchhiking click-bait or hoping for transportation. But it was the rest of her physical appearance that fixed the attention of Kevan Duffy's light brown eyes as he slowed the old Army jeep.

The skin of her face, bare arms, and lower legs was a pale shade of battleship gray. Her hair reached to the tops of her shoulders and was butter-yellow with streaks of ochre. As he drew alongside her, he saw that her hands had an opposable thumb and three fingers; both hands were missing the pinkie, and obviously had never had them. Her eyes appeared to be the same ochre as the streaks in her hair, but glossy, as she took a step toward the jeep.

Foot on the accelerator, ready to stand on it if need be, Kevan loosened the Army .45 in its cut-down holster and quickly scanned the surroundings for signs of attack. These dark days, an operating vehicle, and especially a jeep, was a highly desirable commodity, worth fighting for. In years gone by, he might have added "worth killing for," but since Things Fell Apart some six years ago, everything was worth killing for.

She bent down, her face anxious as she peered through the open doorway at him. "Need a ride?" he asked her.

Her voice was a smoky contralto. "Get me out of here," she said, her tone low. "Please."

No one else was visible. "Climb in quickly," he told her. "No luggage?"

She did so. "What you see."

She was not chatty, and he was not feeling particularly talkative himself. But they were perforce headed in the same direction. He drew a hand over his dark brown and windblown hair, slicking it back. "I'm Kevan. Kev if you want to save a syllable for later."

She did not smile. "Sienne Vhartan."

She gave the name a slight accent, the last name a puff of air after the V.

"French?" he asked.

"Not really, no."

Kevan left it at that. He wanted in the worst way to ask—ever so delicately—about her physical appearance. The gray might be a body tint, applied for some private reason. The lack of pinkies could be a birth deformity; just before TFA there had been reports on X, unconfirmed elsewhere on social media, of birth defects attributed to vaccines that had been rushed into production without having been fully tested. The ochre hair could come from a bottle. Colored lenses surely accounted for the eyes. But he could not bring himself to utter a word about any of this.

Sienne gazed through the windshield and out to the right, her view shifting from one to the other, as if she were watching for something or someone. Kevan's awareness remained high; perhaps her colleagues were waiting ahead in an ambush. Ahead there were nothing but yuccas and mesquite behind which to hide and wait, and these offered only minimal concealment. The few gullies and washes were too far from the road for anyone to mount an attack from concealment. He had stopped for Sienne because she was a woman alone—not a good situation since TFA. Now he had reservations, doubts. He had always thought everyone was entitled to do at least one dumb thing and hope to survive it, and he had to wonder whether he had just done his.

They reached a point where the pavement had cracked and parts of the shoulder had washed away. Roads had gone unattended for more than half a decade, making travel problematic unless one knew where the passable roads were. This one led southwest through what used to be the Texas panhandle, back when there were state lines. Southwest, because he'd heard there were far fewer people, the land being undesirable. Three years ago he had found a long-abandoned mineshaft that he was able to turn into a suitable dwelling. He had no idea whether southwest was also Sienne's preferred direction, and in any event it did not matter while he controlled the steering wheel.

From time to time he gave Sienne a quick glance. She was sitting with her hands folded in her lap, alternately staring ahead and out the open doorway. If she was thinking about anything, it did not show in her bland expression. Seen up close, her skin was a smooth and hairless pale gray, and the ochre streaks in her hair fairly glistened. The shift had ridden up enough to reveal legs worth looking at. If she noticed him looking at them or at her, she did not remark upon it.

With a quick glance in his direction, she finally broke the uneasy silence. "You fix things."

"How do you know that?"

She looked away. "I know," she whispered. He could not tell whether she meant him to hear the response.

"I'm not that good," he felt obliged to explain. "But I can make simple things work, and make basic repairs. Furniture, some machinery." He shrugged. "It's not unusual."

"It won't matter," she said, and this time he heard her clearly.

A small pothole jostled the jeep enough for her to grab the side of the windshield frame. "Sorry," he said, as they left the last of the trees for open scrubland and semi-desert. "This is a bad stretch."

She limited her response to a curt nod.

"I should have asked, Sienne. Where should I drop you off?"

"Where are you going?" she shot back.

A few more irregularities in the road rattled the jeep. "You probably wouldn't know the place."

She considered this. "Somewhere in the mountains. If we stay on this road, we'll be in New Mexico. Southwest? The Sacramento Mountains, perhaps?"

He regarded her with new eyes. "You know that area?"

"High altitude, very low population density, forested slopes," Sienne replied. "A good place to hide from the rest of the world."

"And far from where I found you."

Her first smile appeared: a tickle at the corners of her mouth. She had thin lips, slightly yellow. "I was waiting," she said.

That reply was almost as strange as her appearance. "Waiting for what?"

"For you."

Kevan hit the brakes and the jeep skidded onto the shoulder gravel and stopped just shy of the broken guardrail. The terrain was high desert, seasoned with jagged rocks and dry gulches, adorned with yuccas and the odd ocotillo. A few miles ahead lay an abandoned village.

Sienne looked at him expectantly, patience in her calm ochre eyes.

"I'll drop you off up there," he told her, pointing. "It's completely deserted. I don't think the convenience store has been ransacked; there'll be something to eat, and some bottled water. Anyway, I'm going to stop there and add gas, so that's your port of call, as they say."

"I wish you wouldn't, Kevan Duffy," she whispered, the words light enough to be carried on the breeze.

Hair rustled on the back of his collar. He had not told her his last name. "Who *are* you?" he demanded, his voice rougher than intended.

Her eyes widened. "But I have told you this."

He took a long moment to examine her from ochre streaks to sandaled feet, and back up to those eyes. Now the courage came to ask the obvious, to sum up all his questions into three short words. "*What* are you?"

Her response made no sense. "I am Valangian."

He thought he knew that one. "From Scandinavia. Norway, maybe."

"You are thinking of the Varangians, Scandinavians who settled northwestern Russia. I come from Valange."

"And where is that?"

"About 320 light-years from Earth."

"Oh, of course," he sneered. "I was wondering when outer space would come into this." He pulled the jeep back onto the road. There was nothing more to say, now. A sense of relief set in. He had made a mistake, and it did not appear to be fatal. In a few more miles it would be corrected. There was no question of leaving her in the village. There would be food and water and shelter, with no one to interfere with her, and she could decide how best to address her obvious insanity.

More yuccas, prickly pears, mesquite, paloverdes, chollas. The arid land was full of them. Life always finds a way, even under the harshest of conditions. After considering this, he had to ask.

"What's it like on Valange?"

Sienne almost smiled. Not quite. A little flicker touched the corners of her mouth. "It is as varied as Earth," she said. "Like Earth, we have one large moon, named Boort. I was born on that moon, in fact."

Right, he thought. "How long ago?"

"In your years? A little over seven hundred."

"Sienne," he sighed, somewhat exasperated. But what was there to say? She rivaled Methuselah in age, and came from a world far, far away. So she claimed. She looked like she might be a few years younger than his thirty-four. Aside from a few physical differences, such as gray skin and three fingers and an opposable thumb, she might have been born in, say, Wisconsin. Except Wisconsin wasn't there anymore.

"Why are you going to the Sacramentos?" she asked abruptly.

Suddenly he felt weary. "It's a long story, Sienne, and there's not much time to tell it."

Another mile, and he would be, as the Irish say, fairly shot of her. She looked out at that same distance, but her face held no sign of what she was thinking. Second thoughts began to drift in. He swatted at them, and missed. The best word to describe her overall appearance, he decided, was "comely." By her own admission, she had been waiting for him. Were this a lie, its purpose escaped him. True, he had returned on this route before from the northeast. It was not impossible that she had been aware of this. But why him?

"Because with the proper guidance you can help me return to Valange," she said.

"So now you read minds, too?"

"Not at all. I read your expressions. You are torn, Kevan. Kev. Truly you do not know what to do with me, or about me."

"So this is not about just being with me, then."

"To admit to wanting to be with you as my primary reason for this encounter would be…"

"Tacky?" he tried. "Trite? Obvious? Not to be believed?"

"That's…really not fair, Kev. I knew you before I encountered you. I did not choose you at random." She gazed at the scenery for a moment. "You said there was a convenience store in the village. Why don't we have a soda there and talk for a while? Just talk."

"The sodas will probably be flat."

"That's not a no," she said.

"No," he sighed. "It isn't."

002: Friendly Persuasion

The jeep's gas tank and the five-gallon drum filled—Kevan found it easy to bypass the credit card slot in the pump, once he worked out how and didn't have to worry about getting caught—he fought with himself for a moment. How sensible it would be to climb back into the jeep and take off. There were several reasons for doing so, primary among them that he thought Sienne was as crazy as a "insert suitable simile here." Most likely he guessed she was the product of parents who had both been vaccinated. But he could not account for the gray skin; in the end, that stayed his hand.

She was rummaging around in the store. Already she had gathered together a bag of chips and two plastic bottles of soda; the latter, when gently shaken, still showed some fizz. These now lay in the shopping cart, along with some canned goods, boxes of cereal, crackers, and noodles, and several jars of jam, peanut butter, and spaghetti sauce. She pushed the cart to a table and sat down. A desultory wave of her hand invited him to join her.

While she unscrewed the red lids of the soda bottles, he asked the first question that came to mind. "How can you be seven hundred years old?"

She passed him a bottle, and offered to toast with hers. Yielding, he bonked plastic bottles with her and took a sip. The soda was not flat.

"Seven hundred and eleven, in fact," she said.

"Then we picked the right convenience store. Sienne..."

"Hush, Kev. This is my statement, and my plea."

Sienne had been on Earth for most of her life, observing and listening, living out various lives on all the inhabitable continents. Disguised as a man, she had fought in a Crusade; the English sent her as a whore to service the convicts in Australia; As Grand Duchess Alexandra, daughter of Tsar Alexander II, her plaintive cry for the serfs when she was but six years old eventually led the Tsar to free the serfs some twelve years after she "died" of meningitis. Sienne had led other lives, at various levels of society. Other Valangians had visited also the nations and lands of Earth, starting around the time of the pyramids, in the hope of seeing a civilization develop that was spaceworthy. They had departed at last, so she said, in disgust after TFA, the planet being in their judgment a lost cause. Sienne had remained behind perforce, for her ship—she referred to it as a skip—needed a repair that she was incapable of performing. A repair that it could not travel without.

Kevan gave her his best derisive laugh. "You think I can fix your spaceship?"

"I will prepare you so that you will be able to, yes."

"If you can prepare me, why not just prepare yourself?" he countered.

"The process does not work that way for me."

"Oh, that makes sense." He took a gulp of soda and wound up with bubbles in his nose. "You said you knew me before you had met me," he pressed.

Something he had done half a year ago had gotten her attention, and it had had nothing to do with fixing or repairing anything. Quite the contrary. A family of five, living in a ramshackle storage shed on the plains of Kansas, had been put under duress by a maraud, the members of which meant to rape, rob, pillage, and kill, not necessarily in that order. He had a Barrett in the back of the jeep, along with other weapons and ammo. The Barrett was a beast of a rifle, and if it wasn't secured properly to the shoulder before firing it, the recoil could cause dislocation. He didn't like to use it, but it was great for long-range fire, in this case about eight hundred yards. He picked off three of the men before they figured out where he was. With the M-16 and the .45 he moved in closer. The remaining three men fired at him, but over his head, as he had found a wash that would take him almost to the shed. He got one with the rifle, the other two with the pistol. He also received gratitude and a meal from the family. In return, he advised them to relocate to a place less conspicuous.

Little had he known that Sienne had watched this entire tableau. Nor was he aware that subsequently she began to follow him around, while he performed a couple more similar interventions—he was mad at what had been done to the country and to the planet, mad at evil people who arrogated the power to tell others what to think, say, and do, not only in this country but all over the world. He had been venting his wrath in this fashion, in such interventions, for two years, with occasional respites in the mountains of central New Mexico. On this last trip out, he had grown tired of it all, for it never seemed to do any good. Trouble followed people; they were hard-wired for it. He meant to return to the mountains and wait for God, and perhaps even to advance his encounter with Him. He had had enough. There was no future.

And Sienne stood by the side of the road...

"I'm not that good," he told her, when she had finished her story. "Yes, I can fix a few things, but not an interstellar craft. I studied geology and sociology and humanities. I grew up with weapons, and I worked out in a dojo. I know the names of many of the stars. Sienne... let's say I believe you, that I accept what you're telling me. I don't see how I can help you in your present difficulty. Nor do I see any reason why I should help you, even if I could."

She considered this while peering through the remains of the window. He finished the soda. A bird flew into the store and began to worry at something on the floor, probably some spilled seed. The afternoon air grew hotter. Despite the fact that only about half a million gas-powered vehicles were still operating on the planet, the temperatures were going up, degree by degree. Crime had abated, largely because there were no laws to enforce, and no one to enforce them. Except himself, and maybe a few others, but he was abdicating that brief, futile role.

"May I come with you?" she asked abruptly—in no dulcet tones but matter-of-factly. "May I stay with you awhile?"

"I live in a mineshaft," he told her.

"Yes, I know."

That stunned him more than the realization that she was in fact an alien from outer space.

"I have only one bed."

"There must be a mattress in one of the abandoned houses up there."

"There probably is," he conceded. "We might even be able to rummage up some clothes for you."

She gazed across the table at him for a moment. "You said 'we,' Kev."

And he knew he had lost whatever argument he thought he had.

At one point they had to strike out across the hardpan, because the road he usual followed had become unpassable for a stretch of about twenty miles. Earthquakes were not common in this area east of the Sacramentos, but combined with minor quakes and hard freezes during the winter nights, the untended pavement had eventually become fragmented. He kept as close to the road as possible, sometimes climbing back onto the shoulder, until finally they were able to pass along on a long stretch of relatively stable pavement. They reached what little remained of Artesia, got onto U.S. 82 west, and soon began to climb. The sun was three hours from disappearing behind the mountains, five hours from sunset.

Kevan's arms grew tired from driving; he had been on the road since daybreak. Dropping his right arm to his side, he gave it a rest. Moments later, a soft and cool gray hand clasped his and drew it around the gearshift in the floor to the top of her thigh. The physical contact startled him, but she took no advantage of it. Relaxation slowly set in, a healing process. He gave Sienne a quick glance; her eyes were closed, and her pale yellow lips moved as if she were meditating. What he knew for certain was that his hand and arm had begun to feel better.

Presently she brought his hand back and dropped it onto his lap. "If you let me drive," she said, "I can work on the other one."

With the jeep stopped, they changed places. She seemed to know her way around the controls. When she felt comfortable with the wheel and the pedals, she took his left hand in her right. Kevan settled back, tugged at his jeans to straighten them, pulled the hem of his jersey down, and closed his eyes. Unexpectedly he had come to trust her, and he relaxed. Moments later—he had no idea how many—he was asleep.

They were on a mountain dirt road not far from the mine when he awoke. A drink from the canteen moistened his throat enough for him to speak. He had trouble finding words to say. Finally a question that had momentarily bothered him now returned to the fore.

"How did you manage to pass yourself off as a six-year-old girl?"

"I'm glad you had a rest," said Sienne. "I know you needed it."

"Sienne…"

"Kevan, people often see what they want to see."

"You hypnotized them?"

She shrugged. "Something like that, but far more subtle."

"Are you hypnotizing me?"

"If I were, I'd hardly admit it, would I?" But her smile said she was not. "With Alexandra, the problem I encountered was that she herself contracted a fatal illness. Therefore, I could not plausibly remain in her guise."

He pointed. "Take the left turn."

"I know."

"How many times have you snuck up here?"

"Just three. Once when you were here. I watched you sleeping for a while. At some moments you looked serene, at others, troubled."

She drove the jeep into the mineshaft itself, and parked it where he always parked, out of sight just around a bend, past the heavy quilts he drew and fixed at night to block the light from the lantern. With the ignition off, she sat back and heaved a long sigh, whether of relief or accomplishment, he could not tell. She had a now-what look on her face, but was reluctant to ask.

Kevan got out and lit the lantern, to allow them to see their way around. Sienne remained in the jeep. He beckoned her to the folding card table and to the single chair, and drew it up for himself. She regarded the arrangement with a dubious expression, and finally stepped over to the bed and sat down there.

He joined her, at arm's distance.

"I don't bite, Kev," she said. "Much."

"Is this what you really look like?"

"Such a question! Yes, Kev. What you see is what you get." Her tone almost made this last a double *entendre*. Almost; not quite.

"No tentacles, scales, nothing like that?"

"I can make you see them, if you wish."

"Ah, no. No, that's quite all right." Leaning forward, forearms on his knees, he gazed down at the rough stone floor to avoid looking at her. "We're talking around ourselves, aren't we?"

It was not a question, but she responded nevertheless.

"If you mean, am I going to try to seduce you, the answer is no," she said quietly. "I will not use sex to cajole you into helping me. That would cheapen me, cheapen both of us. You see, Kev," and she reached out to touch his hand, "I know what love is. I've been in love, several times over the centuries. I know the signs. And I know you, enough to be in love with you. If we go to bed, it will only be because I want this, and you want it. Not because I want something from you."

It was as bold and sensitive a statement of love as he had ever heard of. Unwilling to tarnish it, he let it pass. Instead, he changed the subject.

"Where is this skip of yours?"

Sienne removed her hand from his. "The next mine over, about a quarter mile from here."

After he had first arrived, he had considered hiding out in that one. But it was too large, the entrance too gaping for curtains of quilts to be hung, which made it inviting for others to check out. Boulders and chunks of broken rock near the entrance of his mineshaft partially hid it from distant view. Only when someone got up close did they realize it was there.

But her statement had created another puzzle, another doubt, another reason for distrust. He sat up straight and looked at her. "If you can fly it here, why can't you fly it to, say, Arcturus?"

"It only works for short Jumps." Her tone capitalized the word. "A thousand kilometers at most. I cannot leave Earth."

"It sounds like there's an energy transfer problem that no longer enables interstellar travel."

"I suppose so."

"Yeah. So, Sienne, if—that's *if*—I can fix it, I can be made to fix it, then love or no love, you'll leave Earth."

Her voice was as soft as starlight. "Not without you."

And there it was: the bottom line. Not only was he expected to repair her skip, if he managed somehow to do that, he was expected to accompany her.

003: Bottom Line

"You would stay here?" he asked, incredulous. "If I didn't want to go?"

"Yes, Kev."

"On Earth."

"Yes."

"For as long as I lived."

She hesitated. "As to that, you don't know what you are asking."

"Maybe you'd better explain it to me."

What had begun as incredible and impossible now reached the next level up. Maybe two levels. Sienne's people, the Valangians, had developed a DNA-altering substance that prevented the body—any living creature—from aging. She was not talking in terms of decades, nor even centuries or millennia. She was talking about forever. As some computer models predicted that the Universe would last for more than a hundred trillion years, her claim seemed a bit of a stretch. Anyone who ingested the substance—she called it *aquavita*, a term she knew he would understand, even if it was not the actual name—remained in all ways the age they were when they ingested it. Up close, Sienne appeared to be in her late twenties. She claimed seven hundred and eleven years. There was a disconnect between the two ages.

But there was more. The *aquavita* entered the place in the brain where the skills, gifts, and talents resided, however latent they might be, and enhanced them.

"Exponentially?" he asked.

"Geometrically."

Kevan imagined that if he were an artist, he'd be Cezanne or Picasso. Had he a skill at sculpture, perhaps Michelangelo. Math—Hawking and Einstein. His interests lay in other fields that had nothing to do with interstellar spacecraft repair. However, he could fix things. Simple things. Replace a doorknob. Reupholster a Queen Anne chair. Duct tape something. Build a bookcase or a desk. Sienne assured him this so-called gift would be more than amplified enough for him to repair the *Etarre*, as her skip was known. Asked why it would not work that way on her, she explained that her own abilities lay in other fields of endeavor. He did not ask what those were.

Kevan wanted to say no. He wanted like hell to turn her down. But he had to consider possibilities. What she was saying was either true or false, or perhaps somewhere in between. She might have had an agenda the nature of which was in no way apparent to him. In the end, only one thing mattered: the *aquavita* would work or, at worst, would kill him. As he was already considering an end in the mineshaft at some point in the near future, if he finally made that choice, the risk of death by alien chemical substance hardly seemed to matter.

"Thank you," Sienne whispered fervently.

His brows bunched. "Just for that, to be contrary, I ought to say no."

She shook her head. "I could see the decision in your eyes. They glow when you become excited."

"Yeah. When do I drink this potion?"

Sienne demurred. "In time. When you and I are ready." Briefly she paused, and dragged rigid fingers through her hair, shagging it. "Kev...you helped that family in Kansas. I know you've helped others. You're basically an armed do-gooder. I know, you say you're angry about the way things turned out in this world. Yet here you are, doing what you can to ease the lives of a few others, and at great risk to yourself. I have to think about what that says about you.

"At the same time, you were returning to this cave with the intention of ending it all at some point. Frustration, despondence, loneliness...all of those affect you. They affect you because you allow them to do so. But you are an integral person. A quantum person, whole and entire. You are what you are. And you are not suicidal."

"Probably not," he conceded.

"And you are not alone." Her smile warmed the cave. "Not any longer."

His response tore at her. "You're serious."

Sienne slumped, just a little. "I wish I could get through to you. I wish I could make you see."

This was the moment when it was his turn to make a move. He knew what it would mean to her if he did so. Still, he had a choice: stay here, go out there. Here on Earth, eventually, death awaited. He was weary of the travail. Tired people made mistakes. Sooner or later, he would make his. He wished he knew more about Sienne. Did he know enough to take a chance? Was she truly offering him virtually eternal life, an extra hard drive for his brain, and worlds in outer space? That was what it came down to. Well he knew the caveat that said when something was too good to be true, it probably was. Did he trust her not to have a hidden agenda, an ulterior motive?

His hand snaked out for hers, and he felt that she knew his answer in that moment, though he was not sure of it himself. A long breath steadied him while she waited.

"Sienne...I don't know that I can live up to the pedestal you've set me on. I don't know that I can even live up to the plinth."

"I believe in you."

And that crushed all his resistance. For just an instant the world darkened, as if it were the last darkness to pass from him. Then it brightened, a broad stroke of daylight illuminating his mind. Though he could not have said why, now he believed.

"You and me," he said.

A squeeze of her hand clinched the deal. The now-what question arose. In the movies, he supposed they would stretch out on the bed and earn their X rating. But that would imply a reward for his cooperation, and cheapen the love-making. He wanted her in that moment, but he banked those fires. The look in her glistening ochre eyes told him she understood.

Slowly that look became a crooked grin. "Surely you haven't forgotten how," she said.

"I've misplaced my copy of the pop-up Kama Sutra," he told her. "We'll just have to figure it out from the beginning. Sienne...let's go see the *Etarre*."

"I thought you'd never ask."

Kevan did not know what he had expected. Certainly he did not expect a great green egg that might have been laid by the mythological Roc from the Sinbad tales. It stood on four short support pods. The top of it was maybe two and a half times his height, or one foot under the ceiling of the shaft. The skip was also that wide. He calculated its length at forty feet. How Sienne had managed to fly it fifty feet into the mineshaft was a mystery.

"I didn't fly it at all," she explained, after issuing a command to the skip's computer to open the hatch and extrude the boarding ramp. "The process of Jump is simply a transfer from one point in the Universe to another. You might think of it as metaphysical," she added, as they ascended the ramp.

"Or hyperspace," he said.

"Or that."

She preceded him into the *Etarre*. They turned left along the gangway and made for the bridge. There a counter ran the width of the bow, and in front and above it spread a window, or Videx, as Sienne termed it. The view through it was that of the recesses of the mineshaft. Along the top of the counter, several modules waited in echelon. Two of them, monitors, were for communication with others or with the skip's computer, whose name was Lagatha. A third monitor, operated by a projected touch-screen, generated holograms on request, including geographical, astronomical, and entertainment, or images and data onto the Videx itself. Sienne was noncommittal regarding the other two modules, saying one was for diagnostics, the other for internal skip use.

Before the counter stood two captain's chairs that rotated on posts set into the deck itself. Along the bulkheads on either side of the bridge hung murphy benches that might be lowered to accommodate visitors. In the bulkheads themselves were columns of bins, drawers that could be opened and stuffed with whatever. Two of them contained various weaponry.

By Valangian tradition, the starboard captain's chair belonged to the captain, which was Sienne. Kevan supposed that made him First Mate. At any rate, the port chair was his.

Sienne stood behind her chair and regarded him expectantly. He had no idea what to say. To him there was a vague similarity between this bridge and the one on the starship *Enterprise*, except that this one was real.

"Our home?" he asked.

"Our staterooms are aft," she told him. "As is the cargo hold."

He frowned. "Staterooms? Plural?"

"Kev...everyone in the Universe deserves to have one place that is inviolate. A place to retreat to, to think or sleep or read or listen to music. A place for your own private thoughts. At no time will I enter your stateroom without permission or invitation. I expect the same courtesy from you." Now her smile raised the temperature on the bridge. "However, that doesn't mean we have to use both staterooms."

"Got it," he said. "Your stateroom or mine?"

"The galley is just aft of the hatch," she went on. "It is stocked with food and drink."

"Including coffee?"

"Of course. There's a brew—"

Sighing. "I haven't had any in years."

"I assume you're referring to coffee? There's a brewer, and a food warmer. Their operation is self-explanatory, which means I should demonstrate the processes first. Now, have a seat, and watch the Videx, and we'll take a short flight."

Sienne issued a couple of instructions to Lagatha, who acknowledged these tersely. In the next moment, the Videx showed only a panorama of matte black. Rather to his surprise, the view did not change. He had been under the impression that the trip would be short, almost immediate.

Sensing his discomfort, Sierra explained. "Lagatha has put us in a holding pattern in Jump. I wanted you to feel Jump, hyperspace, null-space. This is what space travel is like. Once we exit Jump, we'll see our destination in the Videx. Lagatha, complete this Jump, if you please. And there we are."

What he saw, from an altitude of maybe a mile, was the Mississippi River flowing past what used to be St. Louis, identifiable by the remains of the Arch. They had traveled about a thousand miles. In, apparently, a second or two. It had been an easy journey: no lurches in the stomach, no dizziness or loss of balance, no sense of displacement.

"Is it always like this?" he asked.

"Interstellar distances take longer to traverse," Sienne replied. "But as you see, if you had a mug of coffee, you would not have spilled a drop. Lagatha, please brew a pot of coffee for us, and return us to the cave."

Again the Videx went matte-black, this time for maybe a second; once again they were in his cave. Moments later, the aroma of freshly-brewed coffee permeated the bridge. Sienne went aft and returned a minute later with two steaming mugs. She set one in a little round depression on the counter, and returned to her captain's chair, fingers around the mug as if to warm them.

He peered suspiciously into the mug. "Is this the magic elixir?"

"I would never stealth it to you, Kev. The decision has to be yours. And you should know that it's not about just living forever. The *aquavita* adjusts your DNA, yes, at the nuclear level inside the cell, so that you are also immune to all diseases. You will heal from injuries almost instantaneously. If you want to end it, you'll have to kill yourself, and even then that might not be enough." She made a face at herself. "I skipped a step. Kev, I can microchip you with a device that creates a semi-permeable force field around you. Nothing can get to you to harm you. No one can kill you but you. I'm wearing one, myself."

A wry notion came to him. "So how can we make love?"

She laughed. "I said *semi*-permeable."

But doubts began to set in. Sienne was totally serious about this alien and advanced technology. Being unable to die meant a new attitude toward life itself. The impossible became possible. Uncertainties flooded in as the question arose: if one can do anything, should one?

"Yeah," said Sienne, as if reading his mind. "The very fact that you're questioning the wisdom, the morality of what you're about to involve yourself in, tells me that you'll be all right. Kevan, the most important facet of power is self-control. You will have the capacity, as I have, to hurt people while you yourself cannot be hurt. But you are not the type to go on a shooting spree out of pique. When you shoot, when you kill, it's of necessity—in protection of others, in self-protection." She got up and went to him. Her hand came to rest on his shoulder. "I will always be with you, to help and guide you. Always, my love. Do not be afraid."

He looked up into her ochre eyes, now golden and glowing. "Let's get the *Etarre* repaired," he said.

004: Enemy Unknown

Repair was not that easy. First, Kevan wanted a look at the power plant without the enhancement of the *aquavita*. There were two plants: one for interstellar travel, the other for short sublight runs such as that which had taken them to the Mississippi and back. Both of the plants required Jump capability. The sublight plant functioned for short runs, but failed for anything off-world. Both power plants fit into the housing in a forward hold below deck, just under the front console. Access to that hold was gained through a hatch that fit so perfectly into the deck that not even the cracks were noticeable. To descend, one simply ordered Lagatha to lower the platform.

Illuminative panels in the underside of the deck began to glow as the deck hatch soundlessly descended. The hold itself measured, by Kevan's reckoning, ten feet by fifteen, and the walls, overhead, and deck were a shade of gray darker than Sienne's skin. The housing itself was a box four by six and five feet high. On the side facing him were three lines of what he took to be lettering. Again upon command Lagatha raised the housing. Half-expecting bright light or even radiation, Kevan shielded his eyes in anticipation, but there was only a panel in the housing underside to light the contents. The power plants rested inside their own housings, with more lettering on the sides. The smaller of the two issued the faintest of hums—pouring forth, as Sienne explained, the minimum energy necessary to run the *Etarre*'s systems.

With the power plants now exposed, Kevan crept closer to study details, while Sienne guided him through the components. Already he had guessed that the problem lay somewhere in the transfer of power to propulsion, as unlikely as the latter term seemed to fit the travel process. There was no propulsion as such; the *Etarre* simply shifted from one coordinate point to another in space, with no actual realtime motion involved.

The two plants were adjacent to one another, their housings almost but not quite in contact. Between them were four discrete connections in metalloplastic sheathes, rather like wire insulation but more robust. Lettering on the sheathes suggested purpose. Kevan pointed at them.

"What do these do?" he asked.

Sienne asked Lagatha, who responded, *"The lower two transfer power back and forth. The upper two conduct orders from me."*

"Orders regarding what?" asked Kevan.

There was no response. Sienne apologized to him, adding, "Lagatha, recognize and respond to any questions or statements that Kevan puts to you."

"Acknowledged. Orders greatly vary. I might request information from the GalaxyNet or my own database. I perform astrogational calculations. I brew coffee. Shall I continue?"

Kevan chuckled. "No, I get it." A sigh followed. "All right, then. Lagatha, why are you unable to conduct interstellar Jumps?"

"I have insufficient power."

He walked slowly around the housings, seeking ideas that refused his summons. "Yes. But why do you have insufficient power?"

"That is unknown."

"I've asked her this," Sienne broke in.

"Lagatha, have you conducted the appropriate diagnostics?"

"These yield no useful data."

He turned to Sienne. "Can we remove the power plant housings?"

She hesitated. "I would prefer that you drink the *aquavita* before we do that."

He looked dubious. "Something's wrong here. Something I'm missing."

"Perhaps more coffee will inspire you."

"Lagatha has a point," Sienne agreed. She led him onto the platform. "Take us back up."

The taste of fresh coffee after so long gone failed to improve Kevan's vision, but did wonders for his mood.

While it trickled into the carafe, Sienne went to her stateroom for fresh clothing, and returned in a pastel yellow jump suit fastened down the front by what appeared to Kevan to be a form of Velcro. They sat at a small counter in the galley and made small talk for a while, until she deftly returned his thoughts to the problem at hand.

"I don't understand why you delay drinking," she said. "I assure you it will not harm you."

"But it will create a whole new outlook on life." He said this seriously, but added, "Sienne, I will drink this *aquavita*. That decision is made. But even without its intellectual enhancement, I'm seeing...no, *sensing* something amiss with my thinking."

Her golden eyebrows merged. "In what way, sensed?"

Kevan sat back, frustrated. "Well, if I knew that, I'd have the solution. But I think it's something that is so simple, it's easy to overlook."

She disagreed. "This is technology far, far advanced from yours. That's why I prefer your enhancement."

He picked up the coffee mug, drained it of the last drops, and set it back down close to the edge of the counter. Withdrawing his hand, he caught a finger on the handle, and inadvertently tugged the mug over the edge. It fell to the deck and cracked into three large pieces.

Immediately he was apologetic. "I'm so sorry, Sienne," he said, bending to retrieve the pieces. "Well, at least it was empty."

Her casual gesture indicated the door to a bin. "Drop it in there," she said. "If...*when* we get power up, we can use the mass for energy."

"Nonsense. It's an easy fix." He fitted the pieces back together." All you have to do is..."

He fell silent for so long that she grew anxious. "Kevan?"

He rubbed a finger across his chin. His somber expression suggested deep thought. Sienne waited, a bit of anxiety in her eyes; but she dared not interrupt his chain of thought. Finally he said, "I need to go back to my cave. You can wait here."

Sienne shook her head. "I'll come with."

The walk gave Kevan more time to think. He knew nothing at all about the Jump drive. It was something out of a science fiction novel, or a television show. But he knew how machinery worked. It had to be connected to a power source. Whatever was wrong with the *Etarre*'s Jump drive, the solution rested in that connection.

Halfway there, Sienne took his hand. "You're still pensive."

"I'm still trying to take all this in."

She nodded. "Understandable. In your place, I would feel the same."

"Seven centuries?"

"As unlikely as it seems to you. And yes, I know, only vampires live that long. Once we get out into space and on other worlds, you'll find that in some cases longevity is quite common."

"Why are we going to other worlds, anyway?" he asked.

"To do some good."

He stopped, and released her hand. "What?"

She looked down. "I'll tell you over more coffee. Please, Kevan, don't press me on this right now."

"I'm tired of secrets, Sienne."

"And I will tell you everything," she replied. "But at a time and place. Please, Kevan."

They resumed walking, with him muttering under his breath. When she reached for his hand again, he drew it away. Scowling, she abandoned the attempt. They were still an arm's-length apart when they reached his cave.

Here Kevan moved with purpose toward a small storage box and opened its lid. Rummaging around, he came up with the three items he sought, and tucked them into a cargo pocket of his jeans.

"I don't understand," she said. "What will those do...?"

He bit his words off. "Time and place, remember?"

"Oh, Kev, don't be angry with me. Please."

His mood softened. "I'm not. But please, no more mystery, no more surprises."

"I'll try my best," she assured him. "There's so much for you to know."

"I don't doubt it. Hang about, there are some things here I'd like to take with me if this works."

"*If?*"

"It'll work, Sienne." He gathered up a few miscellaneous items, and handed some to her to carry. He took her hand, and they returned to the *Etarre*.

Having already seen the layout of the power plants, Kevan began a more thorough inspection, focusing on this time not on the plants themselves but on the connections between the two. For comfort, he divested himself of the items in his cargo pocket, passing them to Sienne. He moved carefully, with two sets of gloves fitted to his hands: inner rubber, and outer heat resistant. Lagatha had told him the upper two connections transmitted energy, the lower two, electricity. He did not know which of the four was the culprit. He bent for a closer look, still not touching anything. The search took five or six minutes, and ended with an, "Aha!"

"Something?" asked Sienne.

He did not answer directly. "Lagatha, energy connection number two is leaking energy," he said. "There's insulation missing. Why didn't your diagnostics detect this?"

"*I was told to ignore it.*"

Sienne gasped. "What? Who told you? How could they gain access to you?"

"*I was told to ignore it.*"

"Lagatha...*who?*"

"*Conflicting...conflicting...commands...*"

Sienne forced patience upon herself and her tone. "Lagatha, listen to me," she said gently. "There can be no conflict, for I am your superior authority. There is none higher than myself. Whoever told you to ignore this damage is of lesser authority."

"*That...that is not true...true.*"

"Lagatha, don't shut yourself down. We can resolve this. You and I, Lagatha. You and I."

A long pause followed; Sienne fretted. Behind the power plants Kevan waited tensely, ready to conduct repairs once Lagatha recovered. If she recovered. The assignment of gender to the skip's computer stemmed from the sound of Lagatha's voice.

"I will not shut down."

Sienne sighed relief. "Good. Now think carefully, but only of the name. Who?"

"It was Batavan."

"Who?" snapped Kevan.

Sienne sat back, her legs tucked under. She seemed to ignore the discomfort from the hard deck beneath her.

"Who?" he asked once more, directing the question this time to Sienne.

"He was our team leader," Sienne explained wearily. "He assigned observations and collected data to be analyzed back on Valange. We had a disagreement. He said I was a...he was derisive. Your term would be 'goody two-shoes.' I thought he was withholding selected data from the Emporium—that's our high council—and I told him so."

"Accused him," said Kevan.

She nodded. "He didn't take it well. But I didn't think he would, would sabotage my skip. Oh, goddesses. Kevan, can you repair this?"

"Easy peasy."

Her eyes widened. "What?"

"Sorry. Yes, I think I can. Cut me about three feet of that black tape."

"A meter long?"

"A meter is good, yes."

She did so, and passed it to him. "And this will repair the damage?

He shook his head. "Not exactly. It will cover it up and stop the leaking of energy." *I hope*, he added silently. "You should have a technician conduct the actual repairs." He finished wrapping the electrical tape around the connection. "Now that gray tape, Sienne. About the same length. And stop worrying; it doesn't have to be exact."

"I'm not worrying. I just can't believe the repairs are this easy. No, actually I can't believe Batavan would try to maroon me here on Earth." She passed him the duct tape. "When we get back—"

"Maybe we shouldn't go back." He wound the last of the tape. "Lagatha, run a diagnostic on the power plants."

"The Etarre has been restored to full power."

Kevan opened his arms expansively. "Ta-dah! And that was without a single drop of *aquavita*."

Relief radiated from Sienne's face, now shiny with joy. "Lagatha, set course for—"

"Wait," said Kevan, as they ascended on the platform to the bridge. "First things first. I don't know how long my 'repairs' will hold. Let's go to a repair shop first, one where this Batavan is unlikely to be."

"Right. You're right. Make that Willow Wept, Lagatha, and let's Jump. Travel time?"

"Two hours four point seven—"

"Belay the points, Lagatha."

"...five minutes."

Sienne eyed him up and down. "Whatever shall we do for two hours?"

He demurred. "I'm going to take a shower."

"An excellent idea. I'd better come along to make sure you do a thorough job."

005: Willow Wept

When Kevan and Sienne returned to the bridge, the view through the Videx was still the uniform matte black of null-space. Lagatha informed them that twenty-seven minutes remained on the Jump to Willow Wept. They sat down in their respective captain's chairs, she in the starboard, he in the port, and sipped from coffee mugs. Kevan had the look of someone who was not quite certain who he was, or where. The shower, and the intimacies both during and following, had left him in a bit of a stupor. But the Videx and the blackness of nothing led to his current uncertainty. He was actually in outer space. Bound for another world. In the company of a seven-century-old alien female. He was not sure whether he had won the lottery or become the butt of a gruesome practical joke.

Sienne studied him as if from afar. Her ochre eyes had a remote cast to them, unfocused yet glistening as she aimed them at his blue, though his gaze was fixed to his boots on the deck. From time to time he looked up at her, then away at the Videx, then anywhere else. Finally she had had enough.

"Kevan!" she said sharply.

He shook himself back to the present moment. "Sorry. What?"

"Where are you?"

"I was just wondering that, myself."

Her tone was apologetic. "I'm accustomed to space travel; you are not. That's understandable. You'll get used to it. I will help you, Kevan; believe that. I want this to work." A smile crept across her face. "It's working very well already."

"As long as that tape I installed holds," he said.

"Are you trying to get me to come over there and swat you?"

Now he found a laugh. "Very well, Sienne. It's been a while since my back was scrubbed so thoroughly."

"I mean it. I'll come over there and...oh, Kevan." She shook her head.

He gestured toward the Videx. "When we arrive, what will we see?"

"I hope you don't get vertigo."

"That's not reassuring."

"You'll see the northern hemisphere of a blue and green planet about the same size as the Earth," she told him. "There will be some spotty cloud cover. The two tropical continents are habitable, the two polar not so much. The fifth continent, in the southern temperate zone, is mostly dry rock with a few prospectors trying to eke out a living by digging in pegmatite for gemstones such as aquamarine and beryl. There are also some areas of schist where garnets form. Dehydration is the primary cause of death there.

"What I meant by vertigo is that the first sight of a world a thousand kilometers directly below you can leave you with the sensation of an impending fall. I assure you that will not happen. You're quite safe. But your eyes and mind may be incredulous."

"I'll be fine, Sienne."

"I will catch you, Kevan, even if you are not truly falling."

"Sienne..."

"I told you: I love you. It's that simple."

He sighed and nodded acceptance. "All right. What about the inhabitants? Are there any cultural mores or norms that I might not want to violate?"

"There is no indigenous intelligent life on Willow Wept," she answered. "Much of the population is there, to put it generously, because they're wanted elsewhere. Not that there's a lot of crime; there isn't. Many of those who have gotten away have created lives for themselves, and even have families. But the diverse nature of the population has served to mute much of the effects of cultural differences. I'll be with you to guide you when necessary.

"The male...okay, man we are about to meet was a top mechanic for an interstellar transportation corporation. On Willow Wept he goes under the name of

Ramar Fleime. He now runs a general repair shop for shuttles and skips and other small interstellar craft. For personal reasons he avoids working on commercial vessels."

Kevan pondered her words briefly. "I think I'll just stick with 'man' and 'woman,' Sienne. Unless there's some sort of third gender out here."

"Very wise of you. And yes, there is, but not on Willow Wept."

"We have arrived. Shall I take us out of Jump?"

Sienne looked to Kevan. "Are you ready for this?"

Resigned, he said, "Let's get it over with."

"Don't look at the Videx," she said. "Lagatha, take us out of Jump."

Kevan could not help looking. The world appeared as Sienne had described, but it looked so far below them. His stomach lurched, and dizziness shot through his mind. He kept his feet, but swayed. Sienne's arms held him upright as he turned to confront Willow Wept, now the nemesis of his balance.

Gradually the dizziness subsided. He braced his arms on the counter and forced himself to gaze upon the world below him. Even at a thousand kilometers, it looked close enough for him to reach out and touch. He knew that to be an illusion. He was struck by the similarity with a few scenes from television space programs. A new world before him. Something no one else from Earth would ever see. But the special and unique occasion was lost when his stomach lurched again.

"Water," said Sienne, leading him aft to the galley.

"I think I should sit down," he mumbled.

"There's a bench in there. Try to relax."

"Easy for you to say," he grouched. Then: "I'm sorry. Even though you prepared me, I wasn't expecting the...I don't know, the abruptness of it all, the fact of it."

"It happens more often than not, the first time," she said, handing him a mug of water. "It did with me as well." She watched him sip. "Better?"

He nodded, not quite certain. The bench held him up; he leaned back against the bulkhead. "I'm all right," he decided. "Let's go see Willow Wept. Are there willows?"

"Willow analogs," she told him, as they headed back to the bridge. His right hand still held the mug. "Trees that thrive along riverbanks. But the name is simply the way the UT puts it out." He raised a brown eyebrow at her, and she added, "Universal Translator. The actual name of the world is difficult even for me to pronounce."

"Will I be able to understand people down there?" he worried.

"Oh, yes. The UT goes with you as something like a field around you."

"But you're speaking English," he pointed out.

"I speak quite a number of Earth languages." With a grin she added, "I've had centuries to learn them. Lagatha, Jump us down to Ramar's docksite. And you'd better let him know we're coming, so he doesn't shoot at us."

For two seconds the Videx returned to the matte black of null-space. Kevan felt a very light jostle as the skip landed and the realtime view returned. The *Etarre* had landed in a glen facing a façade of older trees—or tree analogs, as Sienne referred to them. Above the trees, the sky was as blue as any he'd seen on Earth. He found himself eager to go outside.

The hatch opened, the ramp extruded, Kevan took a deep breath of fresh air as he disembarked. Sienne had assured him that the oxygen level of the lower atmosphere was four percent higher than Earth's, and he now believed it. He felt invigorated. A mild breeze blew along the hull of the *Etarre*, ruffling his hair and reminding him that a formal haircut was long past due. His feet absorbed the vibrations of Sienne following him down the ramp.

To his left stood the workshop, a flat-roofed stone and brick structure that might easily contain three skips the size of the *Etarre*. The flat roof was sloped to the back of the shop, a defense against rain dripping down the front. From the back door emerged a person that Kevan believed was a man only because Sienne had said he was a male. About a foot taller than Kevan's six-three, he had hairless simian arms whose hands reached well below his knees. His skin was camouflage green, like a military or hunting vehicle, and Kevan supposed his evolution involved heavily forested areas, where that coloration allowed him to blend with the foliage and thereby avoid predators. Nervously Kevan looked around in anticipation of one such predator, until he recalled that no intelligent life forms had developed on Willow Wept. Ramar Fleime was as alien to this world as he was.

Fleime shuffled forward on short, slightly bowed legs, rather than strode. On his face, also hairless but reminiscent of Neandertals, he wore a smile of greeting clearly directed at Sienne. The smile exposed an upper row of block ivory teeth that sparkled in the light from the white dwarf star overhead.

"You've come at a good time, my friend," said Fleime. "The shop is empty. Although I suspect we needn't move the *Etarre* inside. From what you and," here he finally glanced at Kevan, "your companion said, it sounds like a routine problem."

Kevan shook his head. "It was sabotage," he said. "We'd like to know whether anything else was done to the skip."

Fleime did not question Kevan's statement. "A wise request. Very well, have Lagatha roll the skip inside, and let us see what can be done. Kevan, I am pleased to make your acquaintance."

"Likewise," said Kevan. He tried to shake hands with Fleime, and instead wound up clasping elbows with him.

The three followed the *Etarre* into the shop, where Fleime beckoned to two of his mechanics, and directed Sienne and Kevan to a refreshment room. Kevan noted that the mechanics hailed from the same world as their boss. Sienne slipped a card into a slot on the beverage dispenser, and came back with two mugs of a hot brew that tasted like but was not coffee. While Fleime went to supervise, they sat down across the table from one another.

"Will this be a long wait?" he asked her.

"Did you have somewhere else to go?"

He tried the brew from the mug; it resembled tea more than coffee. "You said you would tell me everything, Sienne," he reminded her.

"Not here; not now." She reached out for his free hand. "But I will, my love. I will."

"I'm out here because you think you're rescuing me," Kevan said sullenly.

"You're out here because Earth is as good as dead," she replied, her voice sharp now. "There are other people who should be out here, good people like yourself, but I'm only in love with one of them, and that would be you. If anyone here is being rescued, it's me from my loneliness. As it will be made clear to you out here, lots of birds fall out of nests, but we can only catch some of them."

He laughed without mirth. "We're bird-catchers?"

"After a fashion. People—and by that word I include all intelligent species in the Universe—often have troubles. You and I may be able to assist. This is where we are, Kev. You and I will fix things."

"What are we going to do about Batavan?" he asked, changing the subject.

"We're going to avoid him, for now," Sienne replied. "We're not going to draw his attention to us. He sabotaged our skip. He's afraid of me, of what I might say or do. He left me to Earth."

"I still don't understand why he did this."

"Neither do I, fully. Yet. Finish your drink, and we'll go see how Ramar is doing."

Kevan found it difficult to interpret Ramar's facial expression, but his voice left no doubt as to his mood and state of mind. He was sitting in his office, a general-purpose device, roughly the size of a sheet of paper, lying flat on the desk in front of him, and he had a dark glower under that ridged brow as he stared down at the data in the screen. At first he seemed not to notice that Sienne and Kevan had entered, but shortly afterward he waved them to his desk without looking up. They poised there, waiting for what was sure to be bad news.

"The fix of the connections with that tape was ingenious, Kevan," said Ramar. "It was enough to get you here." He glanced up. "Had you set course for Valange instead, Sienne, you and he would now be in the slow process of dying, without any possible hope for succor."

A frown lined Kevan's face. "I didn't think my repairs were that bad."

"They were not. But there was another factor which made matters far worse." He sat back and looked up at them. "Jump power is produced by a series of power modules. Full power from all ten modules will take you just about anywhere in the galaxy, although it is expedient to Jump in a sequence of shorter distances. This you know; that is, Sienne does.

"You can reduce the amount of Jump energy by removing one or more modules from the series. To do so would limit the range of your Jumps, and require you to make more Jumps in your travel sequence. Removing half of the modules would leave you with enough power to send you into Jump of average length, but not enough to exit Jump."

Sienne swore.

"In other words," finished Ramar, "you would be stuck in null-space until you ran out of food, or sooner when you ran out of water. Sienne, my long-time friend, somebody did not want you to leave Earth, and to die if you managed to try. You had just enough to get you here —or anywhere at this distance—and bring you out of Jump."

"Batavan," she hissed.

Ramar might have grimaced; it was difficult to tell. "I don't think so. From what I know of him, he is casual to the point of carelessness with regard to giving orders and instructions—"

"How well I know."

The trace of a smile crossed Ramar's protuberant lips. "But Batavan *follows* his orders with specific and fine detail. No, Sienne, I fear someone on Valange wants you very dead."

While a fuming Sienne paced around the office, Kevan asked, "But you can replace the modules?"

"This is being done even as we speak."

Sienne came to a stop by the window. Gazing out at the forest, she spoke in a low voice filled with fury and revulsion. "The worst part is that starvation and dehydration would not kill me. It would leave me helpless and conscious for all eternity.

Ramar nodded. "Right. I forgot. Kevan would die, of course."

"What is she talking about?" he asked, pointing at her with one hand, with his other arm locked and braced on the desk.

Ramar glanced at her. "You haven't told him?"

"Told me what?"

"Not yet," said Sienne, averting her gaze.

"Told me what, Sienne?"

She laid her hand on his arm. He shrugged it away. "Please," she begged. "I will. Just not now."

Kevan shook his head. "Too many secrets, Sienne," he groused. "When the *Etarre* is repaired, take me back to Earth." He walked outside without looking back.

In a spot of sunlight through the foliage, Kevan began to mutter to himself. What had he agreed to get himself into? Where was he going, and why? All good questions. And who, exactly, was Sienne? He had trusted her. *Trusted* her. But why? Yes, she was intelligent, she was extraterrestrial, she was...exotic. Was that enough? Was it worth the mystery? The secrecy? In despair he threw up his hands. He was better off on a dying and dangerous Earth.

Footsteps behind him, slowly approaching. He did not want to see her, not now. Spine rigid, he stood facing away. A hand grasped his arm; he tried to free himself and discovered that to be impossible. He looked down. A hairless hand with splotchy green skin. He had just enough time to register that fact before Ramar whirled him around.

"Sit," ordered the mechanic.

Without waiting for Kevan to obey, Ramar sat. His position on the grass reminded Kevan of a chimpanzee, albeit a very large one. He fought back a smile and only just succeeded. A languid gesture from Ramar gained his compliance.

"I would tell you that she loves you," began the mechanic. "But you don't want to hear that. So I will tell you instead where you are. I know enough of Earth to know it is done for, and that is a tragedy, although one of human making. But you have a chance, with Sienne Vhartan, to go on. How old is she? Did she tell you?"

You're just trying to involve me in this conversation, sulked Kevan. But aloud, he said, "A little over seven hundred of our years."

"It's closer to seventeen hundred," Ramar told him. "Your seven hundred are those she spent on Earth. Is this not so?"

Kevan fought to recover from his shock. "Ah...yes, yeah, that's, that's what she said. Or implied."

"In all those centuries, she has never taken a...what you might call a lifetime lover," Ramar went on. "Oh, she has had relationships, and she has played the roles required of her duties and assignments, but never anyone personal. Not until now."

"You're just—"

"Saying that? She does not need my defense to make her points. I am telling you this because you have hurt her. That, is an offense to me."

"I'm—"

"Sorry? You should be. Even more than you realize. I cannot myself see what she sees in you, but I can promise you this: she would not have brought you out here if she did not want you with her always. And 'always' is a time far longer than you can imagine."

By now Kevan was finding it difficult to breathe. "If that is true, which I doubt, then I am not worth—"

"Oh, I will not dispute you on that score, Kevan Duffy. But Sienne thinks you are. Only the deities know why, but she thinks you are." Ramar leaned closer, and Kevan could smell something like brake fluid on his breath. "You are a stranger in a galaxy, a universe, that is filled with matters and people it will take you a good millennium to begin to understand. Science is different. Cultures and rules and mores are different. There are people out here who would kill you, and justifiably so, if you sit with your bare feet aimed at them. Sienne gets into trouble sometimes for wanting to help—"

"She hinted at that."

"Did she? Kevan, that's who she is. She must have seen something of that in you to attract you to her."

For a long moment Kevan was silent. Then: "I did promise to drink the *aquavita*. It really...she cannot die?"

"Nor can you, once you drink it. For that matter, nor will I. But think, foolish human: you are given, at best, seven or eight decades to do whatever it is that you wish to do. You will die, probably having accomplished less than half of what you had dreamed. Here, there is no end to what you can do."

"It's that important, then, not to die?"

"It's important that some of those whom you try to aid do not kill you." Ramar allowed himself a little laugh. "Not everyone drinks the *aquavita*, young Kevan. Perhaps ten thousand of us, out of trillions. I would not have had a chance to drink it, had not Sienne come upon me who was wounded and dying, and bade me drink."

"I'm beginning to see why you..."

"Are her friend?" Now Ramar barked a laugh. "I'll still charge her for the repairs." He reached a long green arm out to Kevan's shoulder. "The decision must be yours. But you—"

Gently Kevan swept the arm away. "I've already decided."

006: What Now?

Safely ensconced in null-space, Kevan and Sienne sat on the bridge, chairs turned so that they faced one another. Mugs of hot tea rested in holders atop the instrumentation console. Kevan had on his usual jeans and dark jersey; Sienne was attired in a pink jumpsuit that only hinted at its contents. Both wore serious expressions.

"Now what?" he said.

"I wish I could tell you that I had a firm plan, but I don't," said Sienne. "I don't know how this will work. We go somewhere, we see something amiss, we fix it. That's about all I can tell you. I don't have a Go-List, a task agenda for the year or century. There are thousands of worlds out here. People need help."

"Bird-catchers."

"You said that before. It's apt."

"I'll just go get my net."

Sienne laughed, and sobered. "You'll find a lot of apathy out here, my love. Much like on recent Earth. A fixation on the vagaries of life. People look at things without seeing them. Without seeing that something could be done. This won't change, and we cannot change it. Nor should we waste our eternity trying. We intervene where we can, and add a bit of brightness and clarity to someone's life."

Kevan considered this. At last he said, "So...we do what? Land someplace and look for trouble?"

"Something like that. And the term is 'downdock,' not land."

"A whole new language."

"Over time, you will learn quite a few. The *aquavita* will help with that."

"Is that a hint?" he asked.

"I do not wish to nag you, my love," Sienne replied. "But in your present state, you can be killed." Her voice softened to a whisper. "That would break my heart."

"You'd get over it."

She shook her head sadly. "Maybe...not this time."

"Sienne..."

"I don't mean to sound gloomy. I'm sorry."

"So where is this elixir?"

She got up from the chair and held out her hand. "Come with me."

In the event, the process was far simpler than Kevan expected. From what resembled a wine bottle she poured a clear liquid into a crystal flute, and bade him sit down on his stateroom berth. Receiving the flute, he took a deep breath for courage, studied the contents briefly, and went bottoms-up.

And toppled sideways onto the sleeping pad.

He was still conscious, but only remotely aware of his surroundings. Sienne hovered over him like a mother hen. He saw only her face. Her ochre eyes fairly glowed at him; he did not know what that meant, nor at the moment did he care. She was there with him. Nothing else mattered.

He tried to reach for her; his arm declined his instruction. He had the sensation of being alive without the ability to move, yet he felt no fear, only a relief that Sienne was with him and that she would know what to do.

Her voice came to him as if from the bottom of a well, deeper than usual and with a slight echo.

"Your DNA is being rearranged," she said simply. "Let it happen. It will not hurt. It can be scary; that is one reason why I am here with you. I am your rock of normalcy. The other reason," and here she leaned closer to him, to whisper into his ear, "is that I truly do love you, Kevan Duffy. This will not take long; another hour or so. I will be here with you." She took his hand; he scarcely felt her. "Close your eyes and sleep if you can."

Kevan decided not to fight it; not that he could have done that. His eyes closed of their own accord. Dusk entered his mind, followed by darkness.

He awoke to find Sienne lying beside him, naked, on the berth. Belatedly he realized that she had removed his own clothing as well. Her eyes were open, as if she had been watching him—watching over him—the whole time he had been sleeping. If sleeping was what he had been doing.

She blinked. Her face was a few inches from his. "How do you feel?" she asked. Her soft voice made the question more than perfunctory.

He flashed a grin. "At the moment? I feel that one of us should roll on top of the other."

Sienne started to move. "If that is what you wish. For it is what I wish as well."

His hand gently came to rest between her breasts, stopping her. "We have time," he said. "I would like to know what has happened to me. You ask me how I feel. The few aches and pains I had are gone. Aside from that, I think I am still me."

"You control the permeability of your personal force-field with your thoughts," she told him. "Oxygenated air in, and in the other direction your exhalations. Temperature within the field will remain constant. You may touch; you may eat and drink." A bit of color came onto her gray face. "You may choose to allow someone to enter your field."

"There is but one 'someone,' Sienne."

Sienne nestled her head on his chest. "By thought you may set the distance of your field from your body," she went on. "Unless I am going into a vacuum, such as surrounds an asteroid, I set my distance at a micrometer from my body. Should I shake hands with someone, they would not notice the difference. I can pick up coins and sheets of paper lying flat. Everything comes with practice, my love."

"I was just thinking that," he said, and rolled onto his side to face her.

007: Observations

A while later, in the galley, Kevan found himself famished. Comestibles were simple and nutritious. For better fare, they would have to visit a restaurant. Despite his hunger, he ate sparingly, after which they repaired to the bridge. They had attired themselves in one-piece outsuits that sealed ventrally—his pastel blue, hers lemon yellow—and black hiking boots. As they took their seats in the captain's chairs, he wondered whether they were going somewhere.

"We're bound for a remote world called Flick's Chance, or simply Chance," she told him. "We'll select an isolated area where I can instruct you and demonstrate to you how to live and get around when encased in a forcefield. After that, we'll go to a local town, Margoo, and observe."

"Observe?"

"Someone may need our help."

His smile was sardonic. "You sound certain of that."

Sienne shrugged. "It's that sort of place."

"It sounds like the American frontier."

"That's not a bad comparison. People go around armed, and disputes are often resolved personally. Enforcement is perfunctory at best, and usually for the most egregious of offenses. Which reminds me, you'll also need to become familiar with various weaponry."

He shot her a dubious look. "If you and I are invulnerable, as you say, we don't care if someone shoots at us."

"As much is true," Sienne agreed. "But we might want to shoot someone who intends harm to someone else."

He rolled his eyes. "I guess I'm not thinking."

"You're in a new and vast milieu, my love, with variations beyond count," she said tenderly. "You've seen but one microscopic bit of this milieu with Ramar on Willow Wept, and have come away feeling what they call culture shock. In time, this will pass, and each new adventure will be anticipated, and not dreaded. There is one important proviso: those of us who are invulnerable try not to show it too often. We can't be killed, but we can be trapped and held prisoner."

"Simple problems, with resolutions that hopefully are simple, if complicated." He sighed. "Yeah, well, the best plans of mice and men to get laid, and all that."

"That's not quite how Robert Burns said it." She got to her feet. "Still, we have an hour or so to Chance, and since you brought it up..."

Kevan winced. "That's really bad. You're going to pay for that."

"Oh, I hope so."

Flick's Chance was more rock than water, and most of the rock was too rugged for habitation. Sienne downdocked the *Etarre* on the beach of a broken shoreline, a thousand kilometers from what passed for civilization on Chance, and put him through some paces with a Sizz and a quarterstaff. Although initially not proficient with either weapon, he proved to be a quick study, undoubtedly aided by the *aquavita*. On his final practice with the Sizz, he fired yellow beams of energy into all ten targets she pointed to. She also ran him through some mental agility tests related to fixing things as well as a grasp of artistic fundamentals, until she was finally satisfied that the elixir had taken effect.

"It will only get better," she told him, as they boarded the *Etarre*. "It's now a matter of judgment regarding when and how to intervene. That comes with experience, and with observation."

"That's what you were doing on Earth," he said, as they reached the bridge.

"We may have had a hand in a few events," she told him. "Nothing major, though, nothing to disrupt the overall path of history. The fate of Earth, in the end, was what humans did to themselves. Lagatha, take us to Margoo and put us at the spaceport."

In two seconds they made Margoo. After negotiating a modest fee for a private docksite, they walked toward the adjacent town. Of ramshackle huts on the outskirts, the buildings were more traditional toward the town center. Most of these had been designed and built from prefab, and served specific functions.

A plume of smoke rose from a taller structure on the far side of town. "Smelting and chemical processing," Sienne explained. "No complex ores. Copper, zinc, chromium, some iron from pyrites. Minerals are about all this world is good for."

Reaching a boardwalk along the west side of the glideway that divided Margoo, they sat down at a wooden table on a patio. This became their observation point. Sienne ordered tea for the two of them, with local honey as a sweetener. Although Kevan was not particularly fond of tea, he found this palatable. The rolls and butter arrived, and he greeted them with enthusiasm, proclaiming that bread was bread. The first bite told him the bread was a salty form of sourdough, barely edible. He made a face at it.

"It's not what you used to find in San Francisco before all the trouble," she said. She cleared her throat to summon better attention. "Slowly and casually, like you're taking in the scenery, take a look at the two men seated at the table at the edge of the boardwalk."

Kevan did so. "And?" he said, turning back to her.

She shook her head. "You'd better look again. Tell me what you see."

"Well...I see two 'men' because you referred to them as men. They have black hair that looks like a bowl cut; you know, put a bowl over the head and trim the hair that is exposed. They're humanoid, and from here their skin appears to be pale green, almost a yellowish green. They're wearing heavy shirts and trousers, in spite of the heat here."

"Why do you suppose they're dressed that way?"

The question puzzled him. "I've no idea."

"Are they armed?"

"They don't appear to...oh, wait. Bulges under the right armpits, right?"

"Now you're getting it. They're Shalians. They're men, because Shalian women are allowed, even encouraged, to wear longer hair. They come from a world whose name translates as Warren. Now, what else do you see?"

Kevan's eyebrows raised. "There's more? I-I don't know what I'm missing. They're just sitting there talking, like you and I are."

"Let's try it this way: you and I are casual observers, with no special interest in the Shalians."

He understood immediately. "Oh! Who else is watching them?"

"*Précisement*, grasshopper. Who?"

Again casually, Kevan looked around, as if taking in the sights. At first his eyes swept past the man seated at a kiosk on the other side of the glideway. Although the man's head shifted position, the eyes seemed to remain focused on the two Shalians. He said as much to Sienne.

"The man is from Rooiz," she explained. "His attire —yellow cassock sashed by a red cloth belt, and sandals—mark him so. Is he armed?"

"I can't tell from here. Maybe. I think we should assume so."

"The wisest course."

"So we're here to protect the Shalians?"

"And then you ask a question like that." Sienne scowled. "Kev, as yet we do not know who's the good and who's the bad. We don't even know if there is a good or bad here. All we're doing is observing."

"But I thought we—"

"You are here to practice observation. My task is to guide you. Surely on Earth when you were helping or protecting others, you made observations. It's not that different out here...hmm."

Kevan's heart skipped one beat. "What is it?"

"The Rooiz got up and left while we are talking." Quickly she looked around. "I don't see him. And in that outfit he would stand out."

"So what do we do?"

"Nothing. He may have gone inside the kiosk to wee. Or into another shop to make a purchase. Or back to the spaceport."

"There's another Shalian at the kiosk now," Kevan pointed out.

"So there is. Hmm."

Even as she spoke, a green airfoil slowed and stopped in front of the kiosk. Piloting it was a Shalian. On the aft bench sat the Rooiz. The other two Shalians got up, crossed the glideway, and climbed aboard the airfoil. A few moments later it was out of sight.

"Much ado about nothing," sighed Kevan.

"Not so," countered Sienne. "You did very well—"

A running child tripped over Sienne's foot and tumbled onto the boardwalk. Almost immediately a hulk of a man came to grab the child by the arm and yank her roughly to her feet.

"You're not my father," the child screamed.

Kevan judged by the voice that the child was a girl. "Don't treat her like that," he said, and got to his feet. Now he measured the man, who was slightly taller and half again as broad. His countenance was dark, and his dark eyes full of anger. His weapons were out in the open, dangling from a leather harness.

"Mind your own business," the man snarled, and started to drag the girl away.

Still seated, Sienne lashed out hard with her right foot and struck the man's left knee. The joint buckled, he cried out, and down he went, clutching the injury. Kevan suspected torn ligaments. The girl, released now, looked up at Kevan with questions in her vermillion eyes.

The man tried to stand, but his knee failed to hold him A litany of curses followed, most of them directed at Sienne. She drew her sidearm and aimed it at him.

"My companion is going to deprive you of your weapons," she told him. "Interfere with him in any way, and I'll burn a hole through your other knee. You'll be sedentary for half a year. Your call."

He lay still while Kevan disarmed him. Awestruck, the girl stood by and watched the tableau unfold. She made no move to flee. Her lips curled at the corners, the beginning of a smile both righteous and grateful. Kevan completely removed the man's harness. Sienne bade the girl take a chair and sit at the table.

"We won't hurt you," Sienne said to her in a tone softened to reduce fear. "If we can, we'll help you. What was this man trying to do to you?"

"He was...take me back to the ship and with the other children."

Kevan straightened, holding the harness in one hand, his other grasping the butt of his own Sizz. "Slavers," he hissed, and looked ready to take out the man's other knee with a sharp kick. "Traffickers. The scum of the galaxy."

"What's the name of your ship?" Sienne asked the man.

The UT translated the response into a verb and a pronoun.

"Search his pockets, Kev."

But all Kevan found was a plastic card not much larger than an Earth driver's license. On it were printed squiggles and symbols. He passed the card to Sienne.

"Nacle Derv," she read aloud. "He serves aboard the cruiser *Pezzish*." She dug out her percom and tokked it for the Chance Spaceport Administration. When the channel opened, she spoke briefly into it, first identifying herself as Sienne Vhartan of Valange. The name got the attention of whoever was on the other end. Sienne issued a simple direction: Board the *Pezzish* and hold her; gather up all children and remove them from the ship; hold the captain and crew in the cargo bay pending our arrival.

"Do I get one of those?" asked Kevan, indicating the percom.

"We'll go shopping. Leave Derv here." She took the child's hand. "What is your name?"

"Lubby. It's Lubby."

"Right. Well, come along, Lubby. Let's get to the spaceport."

Kevan and Sienne found that eleven children had been rescued, all of them native to Flick's Chance. Held in detention by spaceport authorities were the captain of the *Pezzish*, the first mate, and three crew members. Sienne was ready to eviscerate the detainees, but Kevan gently persuaded her to let the local authorities handle the matter, for this was an offense against Chance.

After turning Lubby over to the local authorities, they entered the office of Adma Magar, the head of Spaceport Administration, who waved them to a small refreshment counter and then to padded chairs. Magar was a slender Chance female, taller than Kevan, attired in a one-piece formal suit in pastel green that complimented her emerald eyes and amber skin. At the moment, those eyes held anger, but it was not directed at her guests.

After Kevan and Sienne sat down, Magar seated herself behind her desk, and folded her hands on top. White showed around the knuckles, indicating her true emotion, but she addressed them with an amicable tone.

"Catching the traffickers in the act does not occur often," said Magar. "Or often enough. As this deed was accomplished by a Valangian and her...companion, I would like you to convey my appreciation to Valange."

"Of course," said Sienne, shunting aside the fact that for the time being she was not in contact with her home world. "If I might ask, why children? They are of no use in labor, even something as simple as weeding a field."

Kevan spoke up. "It's much darker than that," he said, to Sienne. "On Earth, such children were trafficked for...the pleasure of others."

Sienne nodded grimly. "As on Earth, so the Galaxy. Adma, what will happen to the traffickers?"

"Their heads will be placed on pikes around the spaceport, with signs that indicate their offense, as a warning to others," she said. Looking directly at Sienne, she added, "Valange could stop this, or at least much of it."

Sienne nodded. "They could, but they won't. And right now I have very little influence with them." Resigned, she sighed. "Adma, we do what we can."

"You did well today, Sienne Vhartan. The children will be returned to their families. You have our gratitude."

At the subtle dismissal, Kevan and Sienne got up and departed the office for the *Etarre*. Both moody, they did not speak until they were both on the bridge. With no particular destination in mind, Sienne had Lagatha Jump the 'skip into the utter safety of null-space and brew a pot of coffee in the galley. With the Videx showing a uniform matte black, they went aft to fill their mugs.

"Shaken," said Kevan, after they gave each other a desultory toast.

"Yeah. It's lucky we were in the right place at the right time."

"Sometimes that's all it takes. But knowing what was in store for those kids, I just get the shakes. Sienne, could Valange actually stop the trafficking?"

Following a brief consideration of the question, she shook her head. "I don't see how. It's so widespread. The corporations and companies that utilize forced labor also produce many of the goods everyone buys. Cheap labor means more profits. I'm not against someone making money, but...well, but. Cheap labor was one of the factors on Earth that led to Things Fall Apart. Quality of work fell victim to lower wages. Who was going to say no to the corporations, especially when those same corporations contributed so much to campaign funds. That was only one factor, of course. TFA was a concatenation of slow-moving events. In the end, a once-promising people was unable to make it to the stars. Present company excepted, of course."

Kevan grimaced. "I don't like being in a bad mood. I guess somehow I thought things would be better on other worlds."

"Don't sell them short. There are some wonderful and beautiful places where people do get along."

"One bad apple. Is that what you're saying?"

"Lots of bad apples. Lots of good ones, too. Remember Ramar Fleime?"

"How could I forget him? Let's just do what we do, Sienne, and see what happens."

Sienne fell silent. She drained her coffee mug and set it on the counter. Finally she said, "I could do with a nap."

"Is that a hint?"

"Not...at the moment, no." She laced her fingers behind his neck and pulled herself to him. "No, I just... just want to be held."

He kissed her forehead. "What a coincidence," he murmured.

008: Ceremonies

Several hours later the *Etarre* downdocked near the shore of a great inland sea on a world whose name the UT released as Plume. Asked by Sienne, Lagatha yielded up a brief summary.

"Five major but unnamed continents are known on Plume, two of which are habitable. The atmosphere has a nitrox ratio of sixty-nine to twenty-three, with traces of argon, carbon dioxide, and ozone. At present, we are on the larger of those two continents, which stretches from just inside the arctic circle to the equator. The shape of this continent, as you note through the Videx, is roughly that of a molar, with the roots aimed toward the equator. The inland sea before you lies between two of those roots, and you are at the southern region of the north temperate zone.

"Anticipating your query, there is abundant plant life in many forms, and a variety of animals terrestrial and aquatic carnivore, herbivore, and omnivore. Sentient life has not yet evolved on Plume, although there is insufficient data to state that definitively. No life forms have been named as yet, I can only give you some very general descriptions from the few survey reports. Need I go into detail?"

"That won't be necessary," said Sienne.

"If you plan to explore, please record details of any life forms you encounter."

"Of course."

"A pristine world?" said Kevan. He glanced at the Videx. "It seems peaceful enough."

"That's what worries me."

"So why are we here, then?"

Sienne laughed lightly. "It's one of millions of worlds I haven't seen yet."

His eyebrows bunched. "Sienne..."

She raised her hands in surrender. "Okay. We're here because no, I haven't been here, and yes, Lagatha gave me some interesting data reports. She has detected pyridine on Plume."

"Which is what?"

"It's a chemical that does not occur in nature. It has to be created. And it is toxic."

That brought a frown to Kevan's lips as he briefly pondered what she had told him. "But that would mean..."

"*Précisement.* There is, or at least was, intelligent life on Plume," she finished for him. "What we do not know, yet, is whether that life originated elsewhere, or here."

"Or perhaps both."

"Or perhaps both," she agreed. She motioned him aft to the stateroom, where they changed to outsuits—his dark blue, hers yellow—and sturdy boots. Dressed for exploration, they headed for the hatch and the ramp, and descended onto a world neither of them had seen before.

Forests curved around the shoreline, and left only a narrow and sloping strip of pale yellow sand between them and the waves. It was clear from the waterline that only during heavy storms did the water splash onto the nearest trees. Kevan studied the sand for a few moments, and saw nothing but what looked like the tracks of birds—or bird analogs—in search of something edible buried in the sand.

He turned to the nearby forest. Though dense, it did not appear to be impenetrable. With each tree fighting for sunlight, most had grown tall and thin, like potential telephone poles. A few were spreading, rather like oaks, at the margins of clearings. The terrain appeared to be rolling, and rugged in places, and Kevan thought there might be washes, gullies, and even ravines.

The forest was silent save for the susurration of a mild breeze through foliage.

Kevan started to take a step toward the trees, but Sienne's arm arrested him. "Wait," she said, hushed. "Over there."

She was pointing to a large flat rock of igneous origin some fifteen paces away, one that given the geology should not have been there on the sand just past the tree line. The rock was enough to sit on, and the mound of pushed-up sand in front of it suggested that feet had been placed there.

"While fishing," said Kevan, as they made their way toward it. Arriving, he laid his hand on it. "Still warm," he announced.

"It's in the sunlight." She looked around. "Those little depressions might be what's left of footprints. Maybe to haul in the catch. But it hasn't been used for a while."

"The fish might not be in season," Kevan pointed out.

"That's possible." She turned back to the forest. "Whoever fished here is likely in there somewhere."

"Along with other critters."

Sienne laughed. "We're invulnerable, remember? As I told you, we don't necessarily want anyone to know that."

At first Sienne led the way, but Kevan caught her up as soon as there was room to walk side by side. He noticed that some trees had actual bark, but others—mostly saplings—were protected by a flexible coating of what resembled bark but felt like latex. Leaves too were different. On an Earth tree, the leaves were all the same shape. Not so on Plume, where any one tree seemed to have leaves of various shapes. Moreover, shafts of sunlight from the yellow dwarf fought their way through the foliage to energize various low shrubs under the trees. They too shared the characteristic of different leaves. Several of them bore pale violet flowers that suggested future berries. Something about these gave Kevan pause while he tried to fathom what it was. Moments later, it hit him.

"These flowering shrubs appear cultivated," he said.

Sienne beamed a grin. "Cultivated! Thank you. I was trying to think of the word."

"That implies two factors," he went on. "Native, and intelligent."

"I'm not sure I would go that far without more evidence," she hedged. "But it wouldn't surprise me."

A thinning of the trees hinted at a clearing ahead. Instead they found a great basaltic escarpment, perhaps twenty meters high and extending in either direction into the trees. The face of the escarpment was riven with fissures that showed as dark isosceles triangles with the narrow angle at the apex.

"They may be territorial," whispered Sienne.

"If they are occupied at all."

She nodded. "Look for signs of cultivation. And be wary. They won't look like cultivation, and it may be protected in some way. The berries were still wild. This may be more deliberate, without appearing to be."

"That implies competition and perhaps warfare."

"Yes. But whatever these people are, they are not the producers of pyridine. They rely too much on cultivation to risk it."

Cautiously they separated and began to approach the escarpment, still over a hundred meters away. "Humans risked it," he said softly.

"Among lots of other things. And where are they now?"

"Are you saying these Plumerians are hiding from whoever does produce it?"

Sienne shook her head. "No. This has been their natural habitat for too many years to count. Their civilization predates pyridine."

"Civilization," he said dubiously.

"They live in caves. Almost certainly they have rituals and practices, incomprehensible to us." She shrugged. "We're going to comprehend—"

"I saw it, too," he said. His heart beat faster. "At the mouth of that fissure. Of that cave. Just a shadow moving."

"I don't need to remind you…"

He finished for her. "We're here on friendly terms. We want to find out what's going on."

"If we can," she agreed. "And Kev…there's no need for caution. They don't know we know. We'll simply walk right up to the fissure and see what happens."

But as they reached the last of the forest, those plans went awry, as three individuals dropped out of the trees to confront them.

The three were of a physical type. Roughly resembling Ramar Fleime in appearance, they were covered with camouflage green hair except for the cheeks and lips and around the eyes, which were startling gray. Humanoid, Kevan assessed, but with marked differences, including broad feet and hands, all with five digits, the hands including opposable thumbs. Each Plumerian—for such they had to be—stood in a slight crouch that brought them down to the height of Sienne at six feet. None wore clothing of any sort; one was armed with bows and arrows. He—or she—had already nocked an arrow in preparation for loosing it, although he—or she—had yet to bring the weapon to bear.

Kevan and Sienne raised their hands in what Kevan hoped was a universal sign, or at least a galactic sign, of peace and surrender. Following a brief hesitation, the one holding the weapon spoke in a language even the Universal Translator did not understand, so that the words came out gibberish to Kevan and Sienne. Puzzled, they looked at one another.

Sienne said softly, "The UT is not familiar with this language. If we keep them talking, it will assimilate it and we will then be able to understand them."

"So it's not 'universal' then."

She scowled. "There are millions of languages on worlds we've yet to find, Kev."

"I know. Sorry. So: keep them talking. Right."

Kevan held out his hand to take hers, and began to dance around her. Quickly grasping what he was about, she followed along with her own moves. At first the Plumerians gaped at them, scratching their heads and beards, and began to chatter among themselves. For a few minutes the dancing continued, as did the chatter, until finally the Plumerians' words came through the UT. They expressed fear, puzzlement, and curiosity. More words came clearly, and finally Kevan and Sienne came to rest on the grass outside the forest, where they had a much clearer view of the escarpment. The Plumerians gathered around them. In faint but direct sunlight, their hair glistened.

Above them bulky clouds had formed, pregnant with possibilities, and when their water broke, plump raindrops would pelt the area. But the Plumerians showed no concern for the imminent change of weather.

"We are visitors to your world," Kevan told them.

The weapon-holder's eyes widened. "Came you here with the others?"

"No," answered Sienne. "What others are these?"

"We do not know. They must come from another land."

"Or another world," said Kevan.

"You said 'world' before. This means nothing."

"My name is Sienne," she said. "This is Kevan."

The weapon-holder's name was Brooth; the others were Kannis and Pajor. Aside from the weapon, there was little to distinguish them, although Pajor's beard was dark green, unlike the pastel green of the other two.

"This world we know as Plume," said Kevan. "In the sky are many others. The ones of which you speak must come from one of them."

"Do they harm you?" asked Sienne.

Kannis countered with, "Will you try to harm us?"

Kevan shook his head, then realized the gesture might have another meaning to the Plumerians. "No. That is not why we came here. We wish to go in peace, and learn more about your," he started to say world, and finished with, "land."

Pajor spoke for the first time. "We can't trust them."

"That is for me to decide," said Brooth. He sounded as if he relished the disagreement.

Pajor's expression changed to one of diffidence. Clearly he was unhappy with Brooth, but had to bow to superior position. Kevan watched the development carefully. Not all would come up roses with this encounter. If Pajor was the kind of person who would subtly undermine Brooth's leadership, there was no way of knowing the result. Not that Kevan and Sienne were in any physical danger, but *aquavita* was ineffective against first-contact difficulties.

"If we are a problem for you," Sienne said carefully, "we will go our own way and you will not see us again."

"That would be best," said Pajor. He immediately received a buffet from Brooth, and glowered back at him. But he did not put his hand to the area that had been struck.

Brooth glanced upwards. "It is going to rain," he said. "We should all take shelter." To his visitors, he added, "That includes you. Come with us."

As if to ensure that Pajor caused no further trouble, Brooth and he took the lead toward the escarpment. Kevan and Sienne followed, with the relatively silent Kannis protecting their rear. Kevan wondered whether an attack from another tribe was in the offing, but he dared not say this to Sienne while Brooth could hear. Halfway to the escarpment, a deluge began. There was no warning sprinkle, no preparatory drizzle; water simply fell. All too soon it converted the gently rise to the escarpment into a slippery morass that made footing problematic. Twice Pajor fell, and Kevan felt himself losing his balance here and there. Of greater interest to Kevan was the effect of the rainstorm on the Plumerians. Their mottled green hair was soon soaked, and water coursed down their hair to rain on the dirt and grass. Worse, it was clear that the rain had no effect on himself and Sienne, for the force-field kept them dry. If the Plumerians noticed this, it might engender uncomfortable questions.

They reached a fissure inside which Brooth lived. He dismissed Kannis and Pajor, who lived elsewhere, and invited Sienne and Kevan inside. Against the back wall some ten meters away, a fire inside a protective circle of rocks lit the interior. Smoke from the fire passed along a channel carved into the cave ceiling and out the mouth of the cave. Two tepees of saplings stood nearby the circle, connected by a rough metal rod from which hooks hung. A Plumerian child of indeterminate age, seeing Brooth enter, shot to his feet and ran to him, crying, "Amma!" He clung to Brooth like a limpet as he warily eyed the two visitors.

Sienne turned to Kevan. "Mother?" she whispered. "He's a female?"

Brooth set the child down, and he scurried to shelter behind his mother.

"This is Bonder," said Brooth. "She is seven rains old. She has never seen..."

"We are not offended," Sienne said quickly. "As I said, we are here to learn. We are most curious about these 'others' of whom you have spoken."

Brooth stepped further into the cave. Water plummeted from above to splash at the entrance, gather, and flow down the slope. Keeping her distance, she shook herself until she was merely damp.

"Entertain our visitors," she told Bonder.

From a nook well behind the hearth fire the child brought a low square table and set it just at the limits of the warmth that emanated. From the marks on the hard dirt floor Kevan guessed that the table was in its customary position. Bonder then brought four cushions of animal hide and carefully placed one at each side of the table. She then looked to her mother.

"Now the tea," Brooth said gently.

Bonder went to the rear of the cave. Soon the soft clatter of clay pots reached Kevan's ears. Finally the girl emerged into the light with a small amphora designed to be suspended, and four clay bowls decorated with rude artwork.

"She made them," Brooth said proudly. "She fired them, and drew on them, and fired them again."

"Finished ceramics," noted Sienne. "Not bisque."

"But where is the kiln?" Kevan asked.

Bonder hung the amphora on one of the hooks and nudged it closer to the fire. From a pile of dry wood she selected two or three lengths and laid them onto the fire for additional heat. The fresh wood ignited immediately, as if it had been treated with a combustible substance. Following this, Bonder placed the bowls on the table, one to a side. Again a trip to the rear of the cave, there to acquire three small lidded bowls, of much the same design as the cups. These she placed in a neat row in the center of the table, and stood up straight, looking to Brooth for approval.

"Very good," she said. "Now what do we do, Bonder?"

The girl looked away. "They are not us," she said.

"Bonder, they are our visitors," Brooth said severely. "What do we do?"

With a "do I have to?" look in her gray eyes, Bonder stepped up to Sienne, took her hand, and led her to one side of the table, inviting her to seat herself. She followed the same process with Kevan, leading him to the cushion around the corner from Sienne. Then she stood across from Kevan and next to the amphora, while Brooth took the remaining place.

Hands protected by a pad of fur, Bonder removed the heated amphora from its hook and set it on the table, its flat bottom giving it stability. Kevan noted a pouring spout on the lip. One by one, with great solemnity, and starting with those of the visitors, the girl filled each of the four bowls halfway with an emerald-green liquid that gave off just a hint of steam. When she had finished, Kevan started to reach for his bowl, but a cry from Bonder stopped him.

"No. You mustn't."

He drew his hand back, and raised an eyebrow at Sienne.

Bonder sat down. Brooth picked up her bowl, and gestured for Sienne to take hers. Brooth extended her bowl across the table to Sienne. Grasping the intent, Sienne held out her bowl. Together they took the bowls from one another and placed them on the table before them. Bonder and Kevan made an identical exchange. A moment of motionless silence passed.

A casual wave of Brooth's hand indicated the three covered bowls. "These contain herbs and spices," she explained. "You may season your tea with either, but I do not recommend with both. But do not drink yet."

After examining the contents of the bowls, Sienne selected an herbal while Kevan opted for a pale yellow-brown, sweet-smelling powder. Now all four of them raised their bowls, touched them together over the center of the table, and took a sip or two.

"Now," said Brooth, "you may drink."

"Thank you," said Sienne.

"Is this ceremony held for all visitors?" asked Kevan.

"It is our way," Brooth said simply, as if he should have known.

Indicating her bowl, Sienne said, "This is very tasty. What do you call it?"

The UT translated the response as, "Tea."

"Are you hungry?" asked Brooth.

"We do not wish to impose," said Sienne. "You have been very kind to us already."

Outside, the rain fell harder, and the sky darkened almost to night. The air in the cave grew moist. Kevan wondered how long the storm would last. If it endured well into the night, what then?

"This will last until morning," said Brooth, with a look toward the cave entrance. "You are welcome to stay with us."

"You are most gracious," said Sienne. A glance at Kevan got him to nod.

Outside, lightning flashed, followed almost immediately by a peal of thunder. Bonder cried out at the unexpected sound, and Brooth reached out to steady her and comfort her. A little gesture from Brooth got the girl to slide around the table to her. Clinging to her mother now, she sought safety.

"Perhaps," said Brooth, "we should all try to take some sleep, as best we can." She got to her feet, and led Bonder deeper into the cave, clearly expecting Kevan and Sienne to follow.

A smaller chamber was fitted with various hides and furs, some to sleep on, others to sleep under. The aroma of pungent herbs overrode the animal origins of the bedding. Brooth indicated that Kevan and Sienne might take up spots along the back wall; she and her daughter gathered themselves near the chamber entrance, as if to protect their guests. Sleep rapidly overtook them, for they were accustomed to the storms. Kevan and Sienne lay close together, and both started with each crash of thunder. Presently, however, fatigue set in. They closed their eyes and fell into a fitful slumber.

Chill eventually awoke them. The fire had dwindled but not gone out; either Brooth or Bonder had gotten up to throw another log on it. But the temperature outside, in the rain, had found its way into the cave. Kevan rolled over and snuggled against Sienne's back, which warmed his front but did very little for the other side. Finally he abandoned the attempt to find sleep again, and sat up.

The movement roused Sienne, who rolled over. "What's wrong?" she worried.

He found a laugh. "My prehistoric ancestors relished being cave dwellers," he told her. "Me, not so much."

She sat up beside him; stiff fingers shagged her hair. "The rain is letting up."

"So it is. Sienne, we're no closer to learning the source of the pyridine."

"But we're learning about another society, another culture. One step at a time, Kev."

"Yeah." He began to feel morose. It had to be the weather, he thought. It had to be something he could do nothing about. Idly he said, "Maybe it's being dumped into the sea."

Sienne nodded. "Such was my thought as well. We need to ask Brooth about surf fishing and the gathering of shellfish. I'm hoping the dump site is a place smaller and very remote, so it doesn't affect the Plumerians, but if the dumpers don't know about them..."

"Or care about them."

She sighed. "Yeah. I didn't want to say that."

The rain became a drizzle became a mist became moist air. Light began to shine into the fissure; dawn had broken through the overcast. Kevan got to his feet and shuffled to the opening, with Sienne alongside him. The clouds were scudding away, leaving the skies to the rising yellow dwarf.

"Better," said Kevan. Yawning, he stretched his arms.

Sienne's pocket comm began to issue a beeping signal. She extracted the device, tokked it to quell the signal, and checked the message. At Kevan's raised eyebrow, she said, "Lagatha was to notify me if a ship came into the area. It's downdocking on the bank of a river where it flows into the sea, about five kilometers from here." She pointed in the general direction. "You go on.

I'll make your excuses to Brooth and Bonder, and catch you up."

009: Toxic Waste

Kevan trekked carefully through the forest. Vines snagged him, roots made him stumble, and a creature up in a tree muted on his shoulder as he passed below. Before he reached the river, Sienne caught him up, and she had Brooth and Bonder in tow. Both Plumerians were curious, and Sienne had merely explained that she and Kevan were going to check out the river.

Seeing the yellow stain on Kevan's shirt, Bonder pointed and laughed. "Furie," she said. Brooth explained that it was a flying creature that ate flying pests. The explanation failed to assuage the shirt stain.

The soft sound of flowing water reached their ears, and the air of the river nestled unpleasantly in their nostrils. Even before they emerged from the forest, Brooth was concerned.

"This is a bad place," she said. "We do not go here."

They paused, peering between the trees. The mouth of the river lay some fifty meters away, and a ship unlike the *Etarre* had downdocked on the sand.

"Don't you catch fish and shellfish here?" Kevan asked.

Brooth shook her hair head vigorously. "Not from here. No more."

"Sick," added Bonder, rubbing her stomach.

Kevan nodded. "I think we've got the picture. Sienne?"

"Brooth and Bonder, stay here," she said, and tugged Kevan from the shelter of the trees.

There was no point in a stealthy approach, for they were clearly visible to the two people in gray-green coveralls who were unloading gallon-sized canisters from their ship. They appeared to be humanoid, with scaled heads and hands with five digits. Their skin was Mediterranean olive. As yet it appeared that they had not dumped the contents into the water.

As Kevan and Sienne grew closer, they realized that the two were slightly taller, but thinner underneath the coveralls. Having spotted them, the two paused in what they were doing and simply stared, as if they had not expected to find signs of a population on the planet. Neither appeared to be armed.

Sienne and Kevan approached cautiously. He was content to follow her lead, as this was her sort of business. As they drew up to the men—for that gender was the working assumption—one of them said something that the UT translated as "Speakee Englee?"

"What are you dumping?" asked Sienne.

The riposte startled the two men. The shorter of the two, whose head scales were gray, said, "It's just some stuff. You wouldn't understand. Who are you?"

Sienne introduced herself and Kevan, but she withheld her world of origin for the time being. One of the canisters had been opened, and already she caught a whiff of the chemical as it was blown by a breeze over the ocean.

"The chemical formula of that molecule consists of five carbon atoms, five nitrogen atoms, and one hydrogen atom," she said, unperturbed. "It is toxic, and is spoiling the waters. Load it back up. I see your corporation name is Dowdnor. Their headquarters is located on Hegliov. I shall have a word with them about this."

The taller of the two made a rude sound, and gave a wave of dismissal before setting down another canister on the sand. The shorter one said, "I don't know who you are, but I think you'd better leave. This world is uninhabited, so you must be from some other system, and certainly have no jurisdiction here." Having relieved himself of this statement, he went back inside the ship and returned with two more canisters.

As he tried to exit the ship, he found his way blocked by Sienne and Kevan. "Put them back," she said. "Put the rest back. Then leave."

He tried to nudge her aside with one of the canisters. She glanced at Kevan, inviting him now to become involved. From where he stood, there was little he could do except slam his boot toe at a spot just below the man's kneecap. Which he did.

Sienne caught one of the canisters he dropped, and held her breath as the other one tumbled onto the off-ramp. Kevan caught it before it could tip over. He was relieved to see that the cap had held.

The blow from Kevan caused the man to spill to the ground, clutching his knee and the dislocated kneecap. The taller man now moved to intervene, but was stopped short by Sienne's simple statement.

"I am from Valange," she said, almost casually. "This is my assistant." The violence made it advisable for her to draw her sidearm, which she aimed generally. After a glance down at the injured man, she added, "It looks like you'll have to reload those on your own."

"I-I...we did not know."

"Now you do."

She stepped from the ramp onto the sand, drawing Kevan with her. There they watched while the canisters were reloaded. Brooth and Bonder chose that moment to come out of the forest to see what was happening. They joined Sienne and Kevan near the bank of the river.

"They were hurting the river?" asked Bonder.

The two men had stopped to stare. "This world is 'uninhabited' by these Plumerians," Sienne told them. A little gesture reminded them of the canisters remaining on the sand. "Continue working." Belatedly she realized she had a question to answer. "Yes, Bonder, they were hurting the river and the ocean."

Kevan assisted the injured man back aboard the ship and onto the bridge. With his own sidearm drawn, he searched for anyone else who might be aboard. He found no one from Dowdnor Corporation, but in one of the staterooms, a young female cowered on a corner of her berth when he entered.

"Please," she begged. "No more."

She was attired in a simple brown gown ragged around the edges, and held in place by thin straps, one of which was broken. There were traces of dark red blood on the fabric. Her skin, like Sienne's, was gray, but a sad and weary shade of it, as if she needed sunlight to restore its proper hue. Disheveled and dirty butter-yellow hair lay plastered on her bare shoulders. A pungent odor wafted from her, and Kevan decided not to think about its composition.

Lowering the sidearm, he nevertheless retained his grip on it. "My name is Kevan," he said gently. "I won't hurt you."

She blinked lifeless golden eyes at him. He braved a step closer.

"N-no," she sobbed.

"Please trust me. I've got to get you out of here."

"Th-they'll kill me."

"Not if we kill them first." He took another step, and was able to sit down at the other end of the berth. He noted that she shrank from him. "What's your name?"

"Ma...it's Melanne."

He held out a hand to her, but was careful not to touch her. "Melanne, I'd like to get you out of here."

"Please no."

"I mean you no harm at all. I want to help you."

"Kevan?" Sienne called.

The sound of the voice doubled the fear in the young woman's eyes. He hastened to reassure her. "She's with me," he said. "Her name is Sienne. She is from Valange. She'll help you, too."

"Va-Valange?"

He smiled. Her tone seemed to convey a little dash of relief. "The same world you're from," he said, and raised his voice. "In the stateroom," he called.

Seconds later, Sienne appeared in the doorway. For a long moment she stood gazing at Melanne, her expression almost impossible for Kevan to read. Almost, because never before had he seen such fury in her eyes. It permeated her entire face, and made the sidearm tremble in her hands.

Finally she said, "I'll be right back," and swept from the doorway.

For a minute or two Kevan sat with her; then he stood up. "Do you have any other clothes? Or is anything of yours aboard?" She shook her head. "Please let us help you."

Slowly she rose to her feet. Though she was unsteady, Kevan resisted the urge to reach out to her. He would not be surprised if never again would she allow a man to touch her. Wariness mixed with fright in her eyes as she took a wobbly step toward the door. By the time she reached it, her steps were a little stronger.

It's a start, he thought, as he followed her.

They met Sienne as she returned aboard the ship. She had put her sidearm away. Kevan knew what that meant. Though privately glad, he let Sienne deal with telling Melanne.

She did so abruptly. "They're on their way out to sea," she said, her voice gravelly. "Hopefully something won't be too fastidious to eat them. What's your name?"

Kevan started to answer for her, but a sharp gesture from Sienne stopped him. Melanne answered feebly.

Sienne nodded. "Right, then. Kev, I've remoted the *Etarre* here. She's just outside. I have already issued instructions to Lagatha, so you won't have to make any course changes. You'll go to Hegliov on auto and wait at the Spaceport for me. I'll take this ship there. I have... sorry, *we* have a few things to say to some people."

She turned to Melanne. "I would prefer that you travel with Kevan. He absolutely will not harm you in any way. I trust him with my life. But I have some things to do with this ship that I'd rather you were not on board for. If you insist, you can travel with me, but it will be easier for me if you don't. Your third option is to remain here on Plume until we come back to get you."

"No, I...no, no, I-I..." She glanced furtively at Kevan. "I don't want to stay here by myself."

"The Plumerians can watch you while we're gone."

She shook her head. "No, I..."

"Please don't be afraid of me, Melanne," Kevan pleaded, though he was uncertain whether that was the best thing to say. The situation was ticklish at best. She had undergone so much trauma, all of it caused by men. By two specific men, but did her fear carry over to all of them? He waited, knowing she was at least considering her response.

Rather against his expectations, she took a tiny step toward recovery. "I-I'll travel with him," she said.

010: Cocoa and Other Therapy

Aboard the *Etarre* and safely ensconced in null-space on the way to Hegliov, Kevan led Melanne aft to Sienne's stateroom, where he opened the door but did not enter. He stepped well aside while Melanne moved in. "You might feel a little better after a shower," he told her. "Soap and shampoo in the stall, towels are on the racks. There's a dryer for your hair. And you and Sienne are almost of a size, so you should be able to find some clothes that fit you." He stepped away. "I'll just leave you to it, and wait for you on the bridge. Oh, and this stateroom door locks on the inside." He did not add that Lagatha could override the lock, and wondered whether Melanne was aware of that vulnerability.

"Th-thank...thank you," she said, and closed the door after she entered. He did not hear the faint *snick* of a lock being set.

Another tiny step, he thought, as he headed for the bridge.

Soon enough, Kevan dozed off. Not that he was feeling tired, but that in space one slept when one could. Even so, he awoke when he heard the faint hiss of a cushion as someone sat down in the starboard captain's chair. Sienne...but he brought Melanne into focus.

Her hair was still damp, and for the moment a shade darker. In Sienne's wardrobe she had found a yellow outsuit that fit her loosely, and a pair of loafers. Her face fairly glowed from scrubbing, and her skin was now a lighter shade of gray.

Kevan sat up. "Better?" he asked, careful to make it a question and not a statement of approval.

She nodded. "I did not mean to wake you."

"That's all right. I had to see who it was."

Fright returned to her eyes as she wildly looked around. "Who else is aboard?"

"Sorry," he said quickly. "I was just making light, and I wasn't thinking. No one else is aboard, Melanne."

She squeezed her eyes shut. "I over-reacted."

'No, you didn't." He stood up. "Would you like something to eat? Or drink?"

She had a pained expression. "I don't think I could eat anything just yet. Maybe drink."

"How about some hot cocoa?"

"What is that?"

"I'm in outer space," he muttered. To her, he added, "Ah, better to let you taste it, I think." He headed aft. "Back in a few."

"Wait," Melanne cried out. "Don't leave me."

He paused in mid-step and glanced back over his shoulder. "I'm just going to the galley. There's no one else here, Melanne."

"But I-I..."

Yielding to the unspoken, Kevan held out a beckoning hand to her. "Right, then. Come on aft with me." But he kept to a fast pace to avoid her catching him up. Spatial distance between them, he knew, was important. He turned into the galley and began fussing with a mug and ingredients. She waited uncertainly at the galley doorway, an incisor worrying at her lower lip. He decided not to invite her in, lest he push her too far.

A minute later, the nuker *bing*ed. He removed the mug of steaming cocoa and placed it on the counter, and backed away. "Sip carefully," he instructed. "It's hot."

From somewhere she dredged up a sardonic reply. "I would never have guessed." Almost immediately she winced, and apologized. "I'm sorry. I did not mean to be so...so..."

Laughing, he prepared a mug for himself. "I like your sense of humor. It's cool and dry, like English humor."

She took a careful sip. "English?"

"My home world is...or was, Earth."

"I do not know this world."

"It's just as well. You wouldn't like it now."

"Yeah."

Again she saddened, and Kevan knew why: recent life had given her too much not to like, and she was thinking of that. His, "Melanne" brought her back to the present moment. "How's your cocoa?" he asked, a diversion from her darker thoughts.

"It's very nice. Thank you. Is this from your Earth?"

He nodded. "Chocolate can be made into a drink, or candy, or frosting. It's very versatile." He flicked a grin. "But too much of it is not good for you."

It was utterly the wrong thing to say, he quickly realized, for she had had too much of something that was not good for her, and clearly she was remembering that.

"Melanne..."

A haunted look filled her eyes. "What? What?"

"You're safe. Safe with me, safe with Sienne, safe in null-space. We will help keep you safe, protect you until you can protect yourself."

She seemed to hear his words. In the battle to accept them, her eyes darkened to the color of raw umber. He stood by, maintaining a separation of a good two paces from her in the galley and trying not to show that he was nervous. Surely her hurts and sorrows, ended all too recently for recovery, still tore at her and would tear at her for some time. He hoped she understood that, and would fight it, fight for her own soul. Fight to win by overcoming what had been done to her. He recalled a saying from Earth—the best revenge is to live well. Now that the men who had abused her were dead, she could have her revenge if she learned to allow herself to live well.

As a hard frown of doubt slowly faded from her pale yellow lips, she nodded, fractionally at first, then with acknowledgement. "Thank you, Kevan," she said, and he knew she was already taking the first step on the path to victory.

He smiled to himself. It was also the first time she had addressed him by name.

On the bridge they settled onto the captain's chairs, from time to time gazing at each other's reflection in the Videx. Content to wait for Melanne to speak if she wanted to, he drifted into his own thoughts. At the forefront of them lay the question of what he was doing in outer space. The facile answer was that, without thinking much about it, he had not merely gone traveling with Sienne but had also escaped from Earth. He might be the only Earthling who would ever do so. Earth's last great civilization, the American, had fallen prey to those who, not understanding it, had hated it. In his mind, the damage was too great for recovery.

Still, if Melanne could recover, perhaps Earth might as well. It might take two or three millennia of fitful trial and error, but perhaps one day they might develop commercial spacecraft. More likely, they would develop rockets tipped with warheads and once again fire them at one another. In a wager, he would bet that Melanne had a better chance of recovery.

"What was that look?" she asked, still facing his reflection. Her words were clearly enunciated, and her tone pleasant yet curious.

Another baby step, he asked himself. But he dared not reveal the wager he had made, for it might well place too much pressure on her, especially as she had taken but two or three steps along the most difficult path of all.

He tried to dissemble. "I was just reflecting—pardon the pun—on the travel time to Hegliov...which is what, now, Lagatha?"

"Twenty-seven minutes."

The answer surprised him. "Where did the time go?"

"Nowhere, Kevan. It is still here."

He chuckled. "A sense of humor, Lagatha?"

"I am not aware of any. Do you wish me to develop one?"

"Um."

Head tilted and one eyebrow raised, he looked helplessly at Melanne for a response. Bewildered, she shrugged and shook her head.

"We never had this much trouble with computers on Earth," Kevan told her.

"Would you then want to go back?" she asked.

He had to wonder now whether she was asking that question of herself. Whether she was seeking reassurance to ward off an understandable feeling of insecurity. At university, courses in psychology had never attracted him; even the requisite Psych 101 had left him with the feeling of inadequacy regarding the subject matter. Even history, though often a matter of the historian's point of view, made more sense to him.

But he had to tell her something, and quickly, lest she internalize her question.

"It would not be worthwhile," he replied. "I prefer to do things good and useful out here."

Again he knew he had said the wrong thing. Before he could defend his answer, she said, "And am I such a good and useful project?"

The words rushed into his mouth unplanned. Even as he worried that he was digging his own grave, he said firmly, "Yes. You are."

Now Melanne began to weep.

Her tears, he thought, were a blend of joy for the future and sorrow for the past. It occurred to him that many tears stemmed from the same conflict of emotions. The way to dry them was to take another step forward, and another. Under other circumstances, he might have moved to console her. But physical contact from a man at this point might well do her irreparable damage.

"Melanne," he said softly. "I'm right here. You are safe. And soon Sienne will be with us."

Her sobbing abated. "Yes," she said, her throat tight. "Safe."

A change of direction felt mandatory. He gave her a radical *non sequitur*. "I studied geology at university. Not that it does me much good out here, not so far. And the humanities, which may be too geocentric to be of much use."

Faint frown lines creased her forehead as she thumbed away the last of her tears. "Hu-humanities?"

"Art, plays, mythology, literature, philosophy. I wanted something different, to balance the hard science of geology."

"You're talking about abstracts," she said. A note of enthusiasm crept into her tone. "A sculpture represents beauty, or anger. The moral of a story or a play invites introspection."

"Did you attend university on Valange?" he asked.

"Yeah. A long time ago."

"Oh? How old are you?" He winced with the words. Such a blunt question.

But she answered smoothly. "One hundred and twenty-two years old."

He knew the UT had translated her response into Earth years.

"You?" she asked.

Argh, he thought. But he had to answer; he had to. "Thirty-four."

For long seconds she stared at him. Finally she said, "I thought you were in your fourth century." Seeing his expression change, she went on, worrying, "Did I say something to offend you?"

He found a light laugh for her, even as he wondered about the Valangian criteria for determining someone's age. "Not intentionally, I'm sure. Melanne, people from Earth age differently." While she digested that, he added, "More cocoa?"

"Later, I think. Kevan—"

Whatever else she wanted to say was lost in the announcement from Lagatha. *"We have downdocked at Hegliov Spaceport."*

"And Sienne?" he asked.

"She is now hovering over the skylight of the Dowdnor Headquarters building."

That puzzled him. "Why?"

"I am unable to determine that. The hatch is open, but the ramp has not yet been extruded. Shall I make inquiries?"

"No, don't disturb her," he said. "I'm sure she knows what she's doing." He turned to Melanne. "You were about to say something."

"Just...thank you."

"All part of our friendly recovery service." Immediately the words escaped him, he wished he could pull them back, for again he had said the wrong thing. Or so he thought. But he saw a smile play with the corners of her mouth,

"I think I'll have that second cup of cocoa now," she said.

While Kevan prepared the mug, the *Etarre* trembled ever so lightly. The hatch had been opened, and the ramp extruded. He caught the sound of booted feet running up the ramp, and felt the slight vibration as the ramp was retracted. On the bridge, Sienne was speaking, her words too vague for him to make out. He focused on the cocoa, and this time handed the mug to Melanne when it was ready. She flinched with the contact, but did not yank her hand away.

Melanne sipped the cocoa, and nodded her approval.

They reached the bridge just as Sienne closed out a communication. He directed Melanne to the port captain's chair, while he hovered near Sienne.

"I returned their ship," she said.

"That was thoughtful of you."

"Yes, wasn't it." Briefly she surveyed Melanne. "Your hair is damp," she said at last. "And yellow looks good on you. But I think we should go shopping, you and I, so you can have your own things. Which brings up the question of where you want us to drop you off."

Kevan turned her chair around so that he could see her face. "So tell us what you did with their ship," he said.

"Oh, that." Sienne snorted dismissively. "I gave everything back to them."

He glowered at her. "Details."

"Do I have to?" asked Melanne.

Blinking at the interruption, Sienne turned to her. "Do you have to what?"

"To go. Do I have to go?"

An uneasy and pensive silence followed. Kevan wanted to respond, but the *Etarre* was Sienne's ship, and hers the decision to make. Sienne shifted on her chair. Melanne stared down at the deck, waiting. Kevan fought the urge to intervene. Sienne gazed up at him, one ochre eyebrow raised fractionally in invitation.

"She does like our cocoa," he said.

Melanne burst into laughter; after a moment, Sienne did the same. Gradually, the mirth subsided and sobriety followed. Sienne said, "You don't have to go until you're ready. The second port-side stateroom is yours for now. And we're still going shopping." She leaned back in her chair and spoke in a saucy tone. "To the details, then. With their ship in hover mode two hundred meters above the building skylight, I removed the canister lids, then one by one dropped the open canisters to crash through the skylight and into the company hierarchs' office suites. Oh, dear, such a mess. Then I flew here to the Spaceport, and programmed their ship back to a point two hundred meters above the docking slots reserved for the hierarchs' personal airfoils, but I did not activate the hover mode. Gravity works. Oops. Finally I raised the Chief Financial Officer and the Chief Executive Officer and informed them that in the immediate future they will have to find a non-invasive and non-polluting means of disposing of toxic waste. I suggested placing it on a stripped-down obsolescent shuttle and remoting said shuttle into a Type O or Type B star. And I emphasized my connection to Valange and the authority that accrues to me based on that connection, tenuous as it is at the moment. Now, then: where is *my* mug of cocoa?"

Melanne rose to her feet. "I'll get it," she said.

011: A Wealth of Islands

After advising Melanne of their destination and gaining her acquiescence, they returned to Plume. As they neglected to advise Brooth and Bonder not to wait for them, the Plumerians had build a campfire and were munching on shellfish caught further upstream, and garnished with wild savory leaves. A welcome to the food followed a welcome for the return, and the five of them sat around the campfire. To accompany the repast, Bonder—with considerably more enthusiasm than before, conducted a ceremony for the guests. Having taken part in such a ceremony the evening before, Sienne and Kevan took it in stride. Though clearly amazed by what she was witnessing, Melanne had the good taste not to interrupt the ceremony with questions. As all eventually became clear to her, she settled in and ate ravenously, expressing her gratitude and appreciation only after all that remained were empty brown carapaces.

More tiny steps, thought Kevan. Sienne noted the expression on his face and tilted her head at him in a question, but he kept a silent counsel.

"This poison," said Brooth, leaning back on the sand, which clung to her fur, "will no longer be dumped here?"

Sienne shook her head. "But it will take some time, perhaps two or three rains, before the poison is assimilated and neutralized by the ocean. Upriver should be safe to fish. And further up and down the shore—I don't know, perhaps half a day's walk either way, it should be safe. If you notice an unexpected taste, spit it out."

She dug a Palmetto from a cargo pocket of her charcoal outsuit and scooted around the campfire so that Brooth could see it.

"If anyone else comes to Plume to dump poisons," she explained, and poised a fingertip above the only icon on the screen, "just touch this spot, and I or Kevan will respond. Tell us what you have learned, and we will deal with it."

"I don't know how to thank you," Brooth replied. "I shall tell Kannis and Pajor, and they will tell others."

"Thank us?" said Melanne. She held up an empty carapace. "You just did."

Back aboard the *Etarre*, Kevan opted to let Melanne sit in his captain's chair, while he settled onto a murphy bench. Lagatha had been instructed to take the skip into null-space, there to poise and wait until told to set a course. For a while there was nervous silence. In her chair, Melanne fidgeted, restless, as if she knew she had something to do but did not yet know what it might be. Sienne, in turn, studied Melanne's reflection in the Videx, the suggestion of a smile on her lips. And Kevan had no idea what to do with himself.

"I'm bored," he said, in the petulant tone of an adolescent whose right to be entertained was not receiving the respect it deserved. But he grinned as he said it, negating the tone he had used.

Neither woman paid any attention to him. He got up and went aft to the galley, and returned moments later with three mugs of hot cocoa, which he distributed before returning to his bench, there to sip from his own.

"Melanne," said Sienne, and stopped.

"I know," she said quietly. "You don't know what to do with me."

Sienne nodded fractionally. "You need..."

"Therapy?"

"To talk to someone," Sienne went on. "Kevan and I are not..."

"Trained to deal with someone like me?" Melanne shifted, removing the reflection of her face from the Videx. "The men are dead, so you said. What I need now is...I don't know what I need."

"Kindness," Kevan suggested.

She spun around to him. "Why, yes. Kindness. And I need to count, to matter. Not to others, so much, but to me. When I can matter to me, I'll matter to others. I'll matter to you."

"It sounds like you're already on the right path," said Sienne.

Melanne turned back to her. "Kevan said I was a project. But he meant it kindly. I'm not a challenge to be met. I just want to...to do something. I want to have a project, not be one." Her hands shook; she stilled them by grasping the chair arms.

"What Sienne and I do can be dangerous," he said.

"Just being alive can be dangerous," she retorted.

"Then how about someplace safe for a day or two?" said Sienne. "Lagatha, set course for Thalassica, and let's Jump."

The name of the world was provided by the UT. In reality, it was known by a combination of sounds that added up to "Ocean World." Such it was: a sphere of which ninety percent was under water. The rest of the surface was peppered with islands, most of which were volcanic in origin, although the volcanoes that created them were either dormant or extinct. Other islands were atolls, some easily washed over by stormy waves. The climate of some islands was more pleasant than that of others; after Sienne gave Lagatha a list of preferences, the *Etarre* docked down at a small spaceport on Ring Around the Lake, known locally as simply Ring.

A million years ago, the volcano had spewed its last magma, and weathering began. Winds and waves burred the sides of the crater in most places to rolling hills only twenty or thirty meters above sea level. Plants took hold, as plants do. There was vegetation sprouting on Surtsey on Earth not six months after the final eruption. Surrounding the Ring spaceport was a forest of growth reminiscent of a tropical island.

Hot air blasted Kevan, Sienne, and Melanne as they emerged from the *Etarre* and made their way down the ramp toward the pathway that led to the shore of the lake in the crater a kilometer away. Lagatha had cautioned that the ambient temperature was, in terms Kevan would understand, 84°F. But humidity gathered among the trees as they passed, and almost immediately they were drenched in enough perspiration that Sienne threatened to remove her clothing.

"You're only saying that because you have a bikini underneath," chided Kevan.

"I'm not going to undress," Sienne told him. When he raised an eyebrow, she added, with a glance at Melanne, "I'll tell you later."

Melanne glared at her. "Why are you shutting me out?" she hissed. "You can talk in front of me. I'm not a child."

"That's not what...," Sienne began, but Melanne had already turned away, stalking off through the woods. To Kevan, she said, "I was afraid the idea of taking my clothes off would remind her of a bad memory."

Kevan nodded understandingly. "I said a few things to her that I wished I could take back. But she seemed to ride with them all. We didn't fight."

"This is going to be a project," said Sienne.

"I'd avoid using that word in front of her," he suggested.

As they approached the edge of the woods, they heard the sound of small waves lapping at the shore. Already Melanne had stomped out onto a pier and was headed for the end of it, as if to get as far away from Sienne as possible. They stepped onto sun-warmed rust-colored sand. After a long look at the pier, Sienne disrobed. The bikini consisted of a simple top and briefs, both in solid ochre. Kevan's clothes soon joined hers, revealing a pair of pale blue trunks. Out on the pier, Melanne stood rigid, staring back at them.

"I'm not inclined to make allowances for her with regard to our behavior or conversation," said Sienne. "If she is to remain with us, she'll have to adapt."

"Be gentle," he said.

"I will. I feel for her. When I saw her in that stateroom, I-I...Kevan, I lost it. I felt then and now sorry for her. But I can't alter the past. She's going to have to put one foot before the other. Or not."

"She will." He turned away.

"Where are you going?"

He pointed out at the pier. "You should stay here and gray, if that's a verb. I'd say tan, but I'm not sure that color will show on you." Her feeble chuckle faded in his ears.

Melanne's countenance was hard as he drew near. Without a word, Kevan moved past her and sat down at the end of the pier, dangling his lower legs over the edge. There he stretched his arms and yawned, and refreshed himself with a few deep breaths. The water was clear, and he could see the bottom, three meters down. Silver darted here and there—fish, or fish analogs. Most were about the size of his finger. A few dark fragments of basalt dotted the lake bottom, and stood out against the ruddy sand. Dark green splotches grew as if they were escaping from under the basalt rocks. Moss, he thought, or algae. Surely the fish ate it. Aside from the newness of the world and the island and the lake, he saw nothing to hold his attention for more than a few minutes.

Already he was aware of Melanne still standing somewhere behind him. She had not moved, and probably had not even turned around. He doubted her irritation was directed at Sienne. More likely, she was worried in general, and had taken those worries out on Sienne at the first opportunity. Because he and Sienne had no experience in dealing with a woman of her troubles, their saying the wrong things was, as he already had found out, a certainty.

So he waited, and took in the view—the other side of the crater was half a kilometer or so away, and clearly visible. He noticed a few huts scattered at the edge of the forest, and a few people moving about. He heard a board creak, and it took a moment for him to realize that the sound came from behind him. By the time he figured it out, Melanne had joined him at the end of the pier.

She sat well away from him. As he was doing, she gazed across the lake. The top of her yellow outsuit moved with each light breath she took. Out of the corner of his eye, he was aware of her. Sooner or later, one of them had to break the silence between them. He decided that it would have to be him, but he gave it another minute before saying, "Hey, you."

Slowly he turned his head, as she was doing, until they faced one another. Her eyes were red and moist, but she had not yet allowed a tear to fall. With the greeting he had given, it was now up to her to reciprocate in some way. He wondered how she would do it.

Her, "Hey, yourself," both pleased and surprised him. But she did not follow up on the greeting. Having opened the dialogue, he would have to pursue it.

"Come here often?" he asked.

Completely out of character now, Melanne barked a laugh. "This is my first time to Thalassica. I'd never even heard of it before. What about you?"

"I told you: I'm from Earth. I'm just getting to know my way around."

She nodded, and again fell silent. Now she lowered her eyes to her shod feet dangling a meter above the water. Her expression grew bland, impossible to read. She leaned back a little on braced arms. She tilted her head back and turned it from side to side, stretching. Her sigh was just audible over the lapping water.

"She meant no harm," Melanne whispered. "I knew that. I just..."

"She'll be there to catch you if you fall," he told her. "Other than that, she'll let you walk on your own."

She dug an upper incisor into her lower lip. "And you, Kevan? What will you do?"

"I'll keep you from falling."

"Why?"

The unexpected question gave him pause. What did she want to hear from him? But he knew what she needed from him: honesty, wrapped in tenderness.

He kept it simple. "I am your friend, Melanne. I will catch you if you fall. I will listen when you speak. I will protect you from harm. I don't...I don't know how else to say it."

But already her tears were flowing. Against his better judgment, he extended an arm toward her. Instead of shrinking from him, she scooted across the front of the pier and pushed her shoulders against his arm, tacitly giving him permission to rest his arm there while she wept. He let her cry. There was nothing in that moment that he might say to her. He dared not tell her that it would be all right; she would have to discover that herself, if possible. His statement of friendship contained all that he wished to say to her, to reassure her.

In the curve of his arm, her body quaked with her grief and sorrow. Tears left dark splotches on her yellow outsuit. She drove her cheek against his shoulder as if trying to hide her head inside him. Well he knew that the best thing he could do for her now was just to be there while she cried it out. He did not care how long that took.

He was unaware of the passage of time. The only movement on the pier was hers, trembling and weeping. Presently she began to sob incoherent words. He had no need to understand them, or to respond in any way except to hold her tighter and make soothing sounds. I'm right here, he thought and whispered. I've got you. I've got you. You're safe.

Maybe half an hour passed, or an hour. The sun was lower in the sky. Her tears abated. Her eyelids fluttered against him. A shadow fell over them.

Sienne had arrived.

He did not look up at her, nor did he expect to hear any sound from her. A few moments later she sat down on the left side of the pier, behind him but not too close. He could feel her waiting, waiting. Not to be noticed, but in sympathy. Perhaps empathy. She had placed herself on this pier to be present if, when, needed.

Sometime later—another half hour? Another hour? It did not matter—Sienne gently cleared her throat to announce herself. Kevan felt Melanne stiffen, just a little and for just a moment. Her tears flagged. She wiped her eyes, nose, and mouth on his now-sodden jersey. But she did not liberate herself from the security of his arm.

Sienne turned, and laid her hand against Kevan's back, as if to let him know that she was there. Her voice was a leaf on the wind.

"Melanne, I know you can hear me. I'm right here, because I am on your side. I will take your part whenever darkness falls. I will neither leave you nor give up on you."

Sobbing began anew. It did not endure for long. Tears still streamed as she lifted her head to look over Kevan's shoulder at Sienne. Words still failed her as their eyes met, but Kevan felt Melanne incline her head, a nod of acknowledgement and, perhaps gratitude. He started to withdraw his arm, but she caught at his hand and held it in place. Sienne moved around to Melanne's side, not touching her, but close enough for Melanne to lean against, if that was what she wanted.

It was.

012: Interventions

The Ring's sun, a small orange star, its light strained through gathering clouds, continued to sink toward the waves. Sienne broke the soft silence. "There is a small café near the spaceport," she told them. "We can get something to drink there, perhaps something to eat."

Melanne disengaged from Kevan's arm, and the three of them helped one another to their feet. Side by side, they made their way from the pier through the woods toward the little settlement around the spaceport, pausing now and then at a flowering shrub, or to listen to something chatter up in a tree. The brief trek ended at the front door of Wrane's Café.

Inside they went, and chose a window booth, the two women facing Kevan across the table. For the moment, they were the only patrons. A young man in an apron that had seen duty today now approached with a question on his lips, and both Kevan and Sienne reached full alert, sensitive to Melanne's reaction. But she seemed quite calm at the presence of a strange man, and even addressed him with her order. The café did not have cocoa, so she settled for a fruit fizz and a plate of grains and greens, as did Kevan and Sienne.

Outside, a shadow rolled across the forest and took up residence. Inside the café, the lights came on, programmed to do so whenever the level of ambient light diminished to a preset level. The food and drinks arrived. "Storms only last an hour or so," said the young man. After asking whether there would be anything else, he retreated to his post behind a counter and began chatting in a low voice with the cook in the kitchen. Lightning lit the upper sky, the resulting thunder a rumble, not a bang.

Melanne glanced nervously out the window, already spattered here and there by light raindrops. "It's the sky's turn to cry," she said. A smile flickered briefly across her lips at her light-hearted remark. After a very short examination of the full bowl before her, she dug a fork into the mass and began to eat ravenously.

More sedate, Kevan and Sienne ate slowly, their attention more on the rain outside. Kevan almost wished he were out there, as the air cleansed itself. The day was still warm despite the weather. Wind began to sway the trees, but without endangering them. A few leaves fluttered loose. Other than the off-hand remark from Melanne, no one spoke. Kevan himself did not feel like talking; his recent actions had already spoken for him. He considered a change of subject, but to what? Melanne had shown some familiarity with what Kevan said was the humanities, but as yet he knew nothing of the mythologies of other worlds. Finally he set down his fork, his bowl two-thirds empty, and sat back. Sienne's eyebrows raised.

He shrugged lightly. "I usually have trouble starting a conversation," he admitted. "It's probably a curse from having lived pretty much alone for the past five years."

"Alone?" asked Melanne, her mouth full.

"Societies on Earth self-destructed," he said. "Power and control proved to be inversely proportional to intelligence. The damage was irreversible." He released a weary sigh. "It's a long story, Melanne."

"You lived alone," she pressed.

"It was safer that way."

"But you did some good," Sienne reminded him.

"Only in *ad hoc* circumstances. I didn't do anything permanent. And I'm trying not to think..." His voice trailed off as he turned to gaze through the raindrops.

"Think about what?" asked Melanne.

He shook his head, and did not look at her. "I've already said too much."

"That's not fair, Kevan," Melanne said quietly. "You were here for my hurt. How can I be here for yours if you won't tell me about it."

He did not respond.

"Think about what?" Melanne pressed.

He hung his head, and folded his hands on the tabletop. At some point his right index finger had acquired a splinter from the pier, a good centimeter long and half of that embedded. He had forgotten that, to be closer to Melanne if needed, he had dropped his force field. With his other hand he brushed against the splinter and felt it catch on his skin.

"Leave it alone," Melanne told him firmly. "There should be some tweezers in the medical bin aboard the *Etarre*. I'll get it out for you."

For a long and pregnant moment he gazed across the table at her. His voice was the merest whisper. "I helped several people who were in danger at the time," he told Melanne, answering her question. "But it made no difference. I'm sure many, probably most, were killed eventually. Just not then. It's the way it was, where I was on Earth and probably all over that world."

"You tried to do something good, and you think you failed," said Melanne.

"Yeah. Yeah. I try not to think about it. I just got caught up in the words a moment ago. I feel it still, but I'm okay." He rubbed his face. "There's a poem by Omar Khayyam, with a verse that helps sometimes. It goes like this. 'The Moving Finger writes; and having writ/moves on: nor all thy Piety and Wit/Shall lure it back to cancel half a Line/nor all thy Tears wash out a Word of it.' Or so I have to remind myself now and then."

"I think I understand that," Melanne said with quiet solemnity. "Understand, that is. Acceptance may take a little longer."

"I'll pay the tab," said Sienne. "Then let's have a mad dash in the rain for the *Etarre*."

Kevan laughed. "You just want to do something crazy."

"So well you know me."

Once outside the café, they took off running. Laughter was infectious, and by the time they stomped up the *Etarre*'s ramp and into the skip, they were holding their sides in an attempt to control their mirth. They were also drenched, and left trails as they staggered toward their respective staterooms. Sienne's call for them to gather on the bridge in half an hour became an hour. Kevan was the first to arrive, in green denims and a white jersey. He had mugs of cocoa waiting for the women. Next came Sienne, in yellow as usual, this time a full-length casual gown, an ochre cloth belt cinched loosely around her waist.

Melanne arrived somber, as if the gaiety had been too much for her and too soon. Her outsuit was charcoal gray, a hint to her mood. A quick glance at the matte black of null-space in the Videx elicited a "Where are we?" as she dropped onto the port captain's chair.

Sienne did not bother with the mathematically accurate response of "Nowhere." Instead she replied, "We're safe here. And no hostel fees. We'll go back down in the morning."

"So we're not leaving, then."

Sienne frowned. "Did you want to leave?"

Melanne turned to face her own reflection in the Videx. "It doesn't matter. I don't care."

"Melanne..."

Seated on the murphy bench, where Melanne could not look at him directly, he waved Sienne off. Ups and downs, he thought. Had it not been for the recent trauma, he might have thought her manic-depressive. But she had every reason for irregularities in her mood. Patience, he told himself, and kindness, and understanding. But what had brought this on?

He and Sienne exchanged helpless glances. Unasked, Melanne broke in. "You showered in Sienne's stateroom," she said to Kevan.

Immediately much was clear. "I thought you knew how it is with us," Kevan said.

"How it is," Melanne repeated grumpily.

Quietly, and with patience tottering on the precipice, Sienne explained. "I've known Kevan for over two years. He's known me for about a month. We've been 'how it is' for a month."

"Yeah. I thought..." She stood up, hesitated momentarily, and ran aft, her footfalls echoing in the gangway.

A stunned silence suffused the bridge as they watched Melanne until she was out of sight. Seconds later there was the sound of a stateroom door shut hard. Kevan's heart weighed like a stone. He had expected too much too soon, he saw that now, belatedly. But what exactly had driven Melanne to flee?

As if attuned to his thoughts, Sienne said, "Offhand I can think of but two reasons. She's disappointed in you for being with me, or she's reacting to trauma."

"Possibly both."

"Yes. Of course."

"Sienne, I'm not about to sleep with her," he protested. "I'm just trying to...to..."

"Help. I get that. But you've brought some stability to her after her world was rocked. It's a bond. And I'm being seen as interrupting it."

"So what do we do about it, Sigmunda?"

Sienne chuckled. "I met him once," she said. "He understood people, and especially women, about as well as I understand being paid fifty million dollars a year to hit a ball with a stick."

"It's a good game," he argued. "I've played it."

"Professionally it stopped being a game way back in 1994. More to the point, Freud offers no useful advice in situations like this. Kev, she's just going to have to get past this. Past everything. Time is the only answer."

"You're using my argument. But I'm now thinking she needs help."

"Yeah. But she has to want to seek it out. And I can't see her doing that. Not yet, anyway."

A stateroom door slid open. A moment later, Melanne was standing at the entrance to the bridge. Her ochre eyes glistened with tears and outrage. Bitterness made her tone strident. "I heard every word you said."

Sienne whirled so that she faced the computer speaker directly. "Lagatha, *what have you done?*"

"She needed to know."

"Maybe so, but..."

"You cannot heal a broken bone if you don't know it's broken."

"That's true, but this is not a broken bone."

"The principle is—"

"It's *not* the same," yelled Sienne. "Melanne is a quantum person, whole and entire. She's had a bad patch, all of her, not just a bone. You've made it worse.

Stay out of this unless Kevan or I ask you a related question."

Slowly Melanne approached Sienne, while Kevan held his breath. The outrage in her eyes had been replaced by awe and realization. "You said you would take my part whenever darkness fell," she whispered. "And you just did."

"I wasn't thinking about that," Sienne replied, placidly looking up at her. "I was thinking about my crewmate."

Breath fled Melanne. "Is that what we are, you and I? Crewmates?"

"Among other things, yeah."

Slowly she nodded. "If I...seek help, and I...recover, will you and Kevan take me back?"

The responses came simultaneously.

Again a nod from Melanne. "I don't...don't know any...anyone."

"That's no problem," said Sienne. "I had someone in mind yesterday. Doctor Ashnunna has a private clinic on the island of Kokoh."

Kevan grinned. "Her favorite beverage. That's appropriate."

"Where is that?" asked Melanne.

"Down there on Thalassica."

Melanne almost laughed. "You planned this!"

"No. But I know how to take advantage of a breakthrough. Ashnunna is semi-retired, and takes on one survivor at a time. He owes me a favor and he knows it, although he'll still charge me an exorbitant fee." She leaned back and crossed her legs. "You're expected late tomorrow. Make that later today, as it is past midnight on Ring."

"But...but...we haven't gone shopping yet. I was going to buy some clothes and...stuff."

"Which is why you'll be there later in the day. Go get some sleep. At daybreak on Ring, we'll walk the beach and have some breakfast, and wait for a shopping market to open up on Kokoh."

"You mean...you'll wait here on Thalassica while I... I undergo...?"

"No. You won't be allowed to see us while you're seeing Ashnunna. We'll come back when you're ready. You're part of the crew now, Melanne."

"As long as that's understood," said Melanne, as she stepped lightly across the bridge to the gangway.

013: Infestation

"Now what?" asked Kevan. "And why there?"

After shopping with Melanne and dropping her off at Doctor Ashnunna's clinic, he and Sienne had taken the *Etarre* into null-space, setting course for the world of Lanna Lost. Information on GalaxyNet regarding the planet was sketchy. Thus, as Sienne said, the "Lost" part. At one point in its history Lanna Lost had been a rogue planet, wandering through the gravitational fields of various stars. Finally it had wandered too close to a G6 star and gone into an eccentric orbit that, thanks to the gravitational pull of three gas giants, eventually settled into an elliptical one, albeit at an angle fourteen degrees from the ecliptic. "Eventually" in this context meant one point three billion years. Once in orbit, it had acquired a reducing atmosphere. A thousand millennia later, a civilization long since dead had seeded Lanna Lost with oxygen-producing algae and, later, aerobic bacteria and microscopic animals. What that civilization did not know —did not even bother testing because the probability was a point followed by several dozen zeroes—was that the planet already contained frozen algae and bacteria.

Subsequent xenographic examination revealed that at the time of its origin, Lanna Lost had been a developing terrestrial world when a collision with a larger planet had sent it careening through the outer galaxy. All the ingredients were thus present, but for what? Only the few people who, much later, had settled there knew. And they weren't talking.

"Radio silence?" asked Kevan.

"If they have radios. Otherwise, it's a moot point."

Remote telemetry indicated oceans, continents and islands, mountains, lakes and rivers—all the geography needed for life to thrive. And it thrived: plants and animals and hybrids.

"Hybrids?" asked Kevan, after Lagatha had reached that point in her presentation.

"You're asking someone who has never been there, Kev," Sienne replied, without asperity. "I've been told that trees and shrubs and flowers are automotive, and I've seen classified footage."

"Can I see it?"

"If we reach Valange."

"But we're not bound for Valange."

"*Précisement, mon cher.*"

Kevan sighed. "What's our travel time?"

"*Forty-one minutes.*"

"Thank you, Lagatha. But I was asking Sienne."

"*I know. I'm excited.*"

That brought a frown to his face. "How can you be excited?"

"*I am always excited to receive new data.*" Lagatha sounded miffed. "*You like hot cocoa, do you not?*"

"It's not the same thing, Lagatha." Under his breath he added, "Listen to me. I'm arguing with a computer."

"*It is the same thing. You are stimulated by hot cocoa, is this not so?*"

"But..."

"Give it up, Kev," Sienne broke in. "You can't win. You can't even earn a draw."

"The voice of experience."

"Why, yes."

He returned to the subject at hand. "Are any of these hybrids dangerous?"

"Unknown," she told him.

"Can a tree really walk?"

"You saw *Lord of the Rings*."

"Sienne..." he sighed.

She spoke with forced patience. "We're entering a place called 'Here Be Dragons,' Kev. Maybe there's no one left alive. Maybe the inhabitants imported cattle to chase down marauding lilacs. Maybe their communications system needs a part for repair and they expect it to arrive at any moment." She paused, and brightened. "If you find yourself beleaguered by a rampant oak, just flick your Bic at it. It will desist."

"That's almost funny." He turned toward the galley. "It can't be a part for repair, for how would they order it?"

"They'd get a herd of flowering shrubs to form the word 'HELP,' and hope someone with a powerful telescope is watching. Bring me a granola bar, please."

In the Videx, and fifty thousand kilometers above Lanna Lost, the world seemed to slumber even in the daylight half. Kevan visually confirmed Lagatha's assertion of seven relatively small continents, only three of which were located in the tropical or temperate zones. The northern temperate continent was the greenest, and drained by a mighty river with waterfalls. Inviting too were several small villages, some coastal, others inland. One spaceport serviced this continent, and there were pads at other villages for shuttles to land. Lagatha found a plethora of life signs and abandoned her individual count at forty thousand.

The spaceport was located in noon sunlight, and Lagatha downdocked it there. No one made contact with them, or any other attempt to greet them. Lagatha determined that power was still on, not only at the port, but all over the continent. If communication was nonfunctional, it was not due to the lack of power.

At the hatch, Kevan and Sienne hesitated before instructing Lagatha to open it and extrude the ramp. Following a tense silence, Kevan said, "It's safe for us. We're invulnerable, remember?"

"And we shouldn't display that unless absolutely necessary," she returned. "But that's not why I'm not so eager to go outside. Kevan...there are life signs, but there's no one about. I've seen lots of dead bodies before—in the trench warfare of World War I, for example—but that doesn't mean I'm eager to add to that visual collection. I wish people didn't have to die, but that's not my decision to make."

"Valange makes it."

She nodded. "If they want to. Or not."

"I thought you worked for the government."

Sienne laughed. "The Emporium is not a government. They have lots of power, including extraterrestrial, and they issue edicts and ukases that had better be obeyed. But they are a small consortium of the wealthiest Valangians, that's all they are, nothing more. One of their pet projects is to study other civilizations—and, of course, if there is a good possibility of enrichment, to exploit that. I was on contract to them, watching Earth wreck itself over the centuries. It was good work until the civilizations fell under their own weight and incompetence, and I...well, I fell in love."

She drew a deep breath, looked to him for a nod of approval, and issued instructions to Lagatha. The hatch opened to an empty spaceport; the *Etarre* was the only ship docked. Kevan, his own doubts parallel to Sienne's, felt a lump form just above his heart as they descended the ramp. Again he reminded himself that he could not be injured; it failed to assuage his tension.

They reached the bottom of the ramp. Though redolent with brine and salt water from the nearby ocean, the air was easily breathable. Distant sounds of chittering reached them, but nothing resembling words. Or screams. With no other destination available, they headed for the village. Though not primitive, the structures there were simple, one-level affairs of brick, cut stone, wood, and terracotta, all in natural colors. Earth tones, Kevan called it. Although none of the buildings were painted, a few of the outside walls had received a coating of what might have been stucco, in shades of blue, yellow, or green, all three of which clashed with the earth tones.

"Maybe it's siesta time," said Kevan.

Sienne hushed him. "Listen."

The faint sound only just reached Kevan's ears: a sort of electrical humming, perhaps like that of a refrigerator cooling its interior by a couple of degrees. A steady sound, at a steady volume. It seemed to permeate the village. He looked around, saw movement in a window, and had to look again to believe his eyes. A tug at Sienne's elbow swung her around.

The door to that house opened. An olive-skinned woman in a white jumpsuit and black apron beckoned to them, so furiously that Kevan wondered whether her arm would break. The woman's urgency sent him and Sienne running to the house. The woman stepped back to allow them passage, then sealed the door shut.

The house smelled of freshy-baked bread, ambrosia to Kevan's nose. Bits of flour festooned the woman's clothing. She stared at them for a few seconds, and said, "Starwinders?" in a gravelly but modulated tone.

"We just arrived," said Sienna, and introduced them.

"Bahawa," said the woman, jabbing a floury thumb at her chest. "Come on inside, and don't make too much noise." She did not explain what "too much" meant. She motioned them to a table on which rested a plate of rolls covered by a transparent wrap, and accompanied by what could only be butter, even if it was slightly greenish. "It's all we have," she explained, motioning them to wooden chairs. "That's what we are down to. Most of the other foodstuffs are exhausted now. It's been almost a quarter-year."

"If that's all the food you have," said Kevan, "Perhaps we had better not accept your offer, kind as it is."

Bahawa shook her head. "That is not our way. Together we survive longer than individually. Please, eat your fill. I do have water." She went to the cooler and withdrew a stoneware pitcher and two mugs. Ice cubes clacked as she poured. "Here you are. Where do you heil from, if I may ask?"

"I am from Earth," Kevan told her. "She heils from Valange."

"Valange," Bahawa repeated, a sour taste in her mouth. "No offense, but Valange was unhelpful. They recommended sharp sturdy knives about this long." She held her hands about twenty inches apart. "That's the worst thing we could do. It was tried early on, and probably led to this." She made a face as she sat down. "I'm sorry. You're Starwinders. It's so unlikely you would know. It's the zeleens, you see. They are ravenous." She studied the questions in their eyes. "Zeleens? They are anywhere from ten to twenty meters long, about as big around as your arm, and they supplement their usual diet with meat. They have devoured almost every meat animal on this continent except, well, us."

"Snakes?" asked Kevan.

Sienne shook her head. "I think she's talking about vines. Traveling predatory vines."

"Cutting them into smaller pieces would only enable them to take root," said Bahawa. "If only the monsoon would come, we'd be all right, but it's late this year, very late, and it may not come at all."

"You reached Valange," Sienne pointed out. "Why didn't you send out a distress signal?"

"We had to divert almost all power to the defenses," she replied. "Only one house in eight has power for the coolers and the cookers—fortunately for you, although no one will tell us how much longer that will last. Resupply and commercial vessels are not due until early next year. We won't be here then."

"Can't you evacuate?" asked Kevan.

"There are fifteen hundred souls here in Seaside. Will they fit aboard your vessel?"

Sienne sighed, not wanting to give the obvious answer. "These rolls are delicious," she said.

"I ran out of jam last week, or I'd offer you some."

Kevan turned to Sienne. "We have food aboard the *Etarre*. It might make some difference. And we can get some people off-planet, though I don't know whereto."

Sienne shook her head. "I'm missing something."

"Herbicide?" he asked.

"No way. Remember Agent Orange? Remember the cancer scandal regarding Rodeo?"

"You mean Roundup?"

She nodded absently. "We have to think of something else. Bahawa, what is the usual habitat for these zeleens?"

"Upper Shadda. That's this continent. But the zeleens travel in one great herd."

"Like wildebeest," said Kevan.

Bahawa looked dubious. "I suppose so. And that whole herd has surrounded Seaside. Only the sonic fence is keeping them out. "

"How do they travel?" asked Sienne. "On the ground, like snakes?"

"Not...exactly. They writhe together in a great mass that progresses in the right direction."

"It's too bad you disposed of all that pyridine," he told Sienne.

"Wrecking the environment isn't the answer." She touched his hand, temporizing. "I know that's not what you meant. Bahawa, do the zeleens have any natural enemies?"

"A dubna tree will sometimes pluck one or two for a snack. Otherwise, only each other, when food becomes very scarce. But the power for the fence will be exhausted before they reach that self-consumptive point."

"I'm still missing something," said Sienne, looking out the window now as if the answer hovered there. "What kills plants?"

"I killed a cactus once," said Kevan. "I neglected to water it."

"Bahawa, will the zeleens desiccate if the monsoons don't come?"

She nodded. "Probably. But again the power will last, I'm told, for another ten days at best."

"We could hook up the *Etarre* to the power source," he suggested.

"Yeah. That would buy some time, but it could mean isolating us here as well, plus depriving us of the option to evacuate at least some people."

"Fire," he said. "But how would you direct it, control it? Burning the forest down, and perhaps even the buildings...I just don't see it." Laughing, he added, "I don't suppose there are any volcanoes around here."

"There are three or four on the north coast," said Bahawa. "None here on the south."

Sienne looked as if she wanted to cry from frustration. Not every problem has a simple solution, but this one did not appear even to have any difficult ones. "Fifteen hundred people," she mused. "I suppose we could shuttle them all to another continent."

Bahawa nodded reluctantly. "As a last resort. Better to lose a house than a life."

Kevan took another roll, and smeared it with butter. "These are addictive," he said. He brightened. "Do we know enough about chemicals or substances necessary for zeleen health? Perhaps if we can deprive them of...oh, wait a minute." He snapped his fingers a couple of times. "We're going about this the wrong way. Instead of depriving them of a nutrient, we could find something they can't stand too much of. Bahawa, you said the monsoons had failed to arrive. What do they do?"

She looked puzzled, as if everyone knew what monsoons did. "They produce a lot of rain," she said. "They flood the land. The waters stay for many days."

"But...you seem to attribute defense against the zeleens to these storms," he pressed. "What happens to them?"

"Well, they...they drown, of course."

Kevan sat back. Sienne's ochre eyes glowed; she saw where this was going. But how to bring the rains? She voiced the question.

Kevan shook his head. "We don't have to have rain," he pointed out. "All we have to do is introduce the zeleens to water."

Sienne gazed blankly at him.

"Water," he said gently. "As in oceans."

"I still don't see how."

"Mohammed to the mountain," he replied. "I'll be the bait. Bahawa, can I get through this sonic fence from the inside?" She nodded. "And the ocean is half a kilometer away? If I can't outrun a herd of slithery plants, I'm not trying. All I need is a long pier."

"There are several," said Bahawa. "But..."

He started to rise. Sienne's hand stayed him. "Kevan, wait. You don't know what—"

"But I do," he said, and added with a quick glance at Bahawa, "We can't discuss it, you said. So I'm counting on you, which is why I won't say goodbye." He kissed her, and dashed off, the sound of his name in her voice echoing in his ears.

Outside, and toward the ocean. Humming of sonics in his ears. Weaving a path between houses and huts. Boats visible now, but the full view of them blocked by a writhing green mass. It reminded him of great strands of cooked vegetarian spaghetti noodles. From fifty meters away, now, they appeared to have formed a low barrier in either direction around the village, as close to the sonic fence as they dared. Nourishment awaited them on the other side, and they meant to have it. He wondered whether they knew or somehow sensed that the fence could not long endure.

Approaching the barrier, Kevan did not slow. Already he could see that the strip of zeleens was no more than ten paces wide, and in some places only half that. He diverted his path to one of those lesser strips. Five, six running paces. Surely he could get through that. It helped his attitude to know that he could not die trying. He also knew, that if his plan worked, there were worse things than death.

He stepped right through the fence without feeling it. Under his boots, something squished. Six running squishy paces. The injured zeleens made no protest except to turn on him. He was too fast for them to snag. And then he was in the clear, racing toward the waves and a pier.

He marked a mental checklist: stage one completed.

A glance over his shoulder. A great mass of writhing green spaghetti was surging toward him. Hundreds...no, thousands of strands, gathering together from all around the village, ravenous, little toothy mouths opening and closing in anticipation, seeking food they did not know they could not have. Their green formed a stark horizon against the blue of the sky.

Ahead the pier. The mass was now ten meters behind him. He slowed, just a little, to egg them on. Neener neener. He barked a crazy laugh at the absurd. The wood of the pier sounded hollow as he stomped along it. Thirty meters to the end of it, and he wondered why he had been thinking in metric. Not that it mattered. It took his mind off the voracious zeleens sensing victory and a meal.

Kevan dove into the waves.

But he wasn't sinking as he had planned. He was floating. The envelope of air between his skin and the force field protecting him was keeping him buoyant. Incongruously the word reminded him of an old television show, with Betty White. Told that someone was clairvoyant, she replied that the person was lucky, because she herself sank like a stone.

Only he wasn't sinking. He was being engulfed by a weighty mass of green spaghetti...and now he was sinking, just a little. The zeleens showed no ability to swim, as he had expected. But he had to be totally immersed, as deep as possible in the waters. And there was only one way to accomplish that: alter the permeability of the force field around him. He issued the necessary thought commands.

Now he began to sink in earnest. Air leaked out, water leaked in. It chilled him. Sinking, plummeting, the mass weighing him down now, he held his breath. Held it for as long as possible. His chest ached, his ribs argued vehemently in their attempt to expand and draw a fresh breath. He had no idea how deep he was. He hoped it would be enough. It had to be enough, it had to.

The mass weighed him down to the muddy bottom. Thirty meters, forty? More? Bubbles emerged from his mouth; he was unable to prevent their escape. Dimly he was aware that some of zeleens had ceased to move. That gave him scant comfort. He was compelled to surrender to his rib cage. Water rushed into his lungs. He lay on the muddy bottom in darkness brought on by the blanket of zeleens. Some still tried to tear at him, without success.

Another darkness began to set in, to blanket his mind. He fought for oxygen, and got more water instead. His limbs enfeebled now, he felt himself relax. A passing, final thought formed...

"Now it's up to..." But that thought died, stillborn and incomplete, and there was only the ultimate envelopment of darkness itself.

014: Search and Rescue

Sienne gave Kevan ten minutes before she panicked, and another ten—fidgeting and pacing Bahawa's front room—before she yielded to the urge to go after him. They had worked together long enough for her to deduce what he had in mind. There was only one risk, but it was huge: she had to find him.

No zeleens chased her as she dashed out to the pier. All around her in the water floated thousands of lifeless green spaghetti noodles. Already the blooks, graffigs, and turklets—herbivorous fish analogs all—had begun to feast on this cornucopia. As she ran out to the end of the pier, she saw the jerks and spasms as the fish tore at the viny plants. She had no time to pause and watch. Kevan had to be somewhere below. The sheer mass of zeleens would not have allowed him to swim away.

After expanding her air capacity in the force field, she dove into the green mass in the waves. The great majority of the strands were limp, lifeless; many bore signs of having been fed on. She fought her way through them. It was rough going, for the force field was not capable of labor, but protection. Bubbles of carbon dioxide rose to the surface, as the force field around her had been rendered permeable to her exhalation. Down she forced herself, disentangling her limbs from the vines that impeded her progress. How deep had he gone? To the bottom? It seemed impossible to reach him through the dead plant matter. She was fighting both plants and buoyancy, the latter a factor she had not considered. But she knew that Kevan had considered it. His response to the problem terrified her. If she was unable to locate him, he would remain in limbo even after the planet itself had disintegrated.

If only she and he were telepathic. But that would not have helped, with him unconscious. A new problem arose. Given that she could locate him, she would have to drag him up through the mass of vegetation. The buoyancy that now created difficulties for her might then be advantageous. If she found him.

Sunlight barely reached through the dead vines. Sienne had to feel her way for the bottom, where surely he now lay. Where, damn it, where, where? Her reaching hands immersed themselves in mud. She felt a few shells, some rocks. At least the force field enabled her to keep her eyes open. But there was nothing save green cooked spaghetti to see, nothing! He had to be somewhere...

A dark shape on the bottom. A boulder? A rise of mud, with some predator lurking under it? Closer she swam through the tangles; she had no need of caution. Kevan? She shoved her hand at the shape, but she was unable to touch it directly. Because of the force field around it.

Heart a-stutter now, she clutched at him, grasping his ankle. The mass of vines formed a formidable barrier above her. Another problem joined it: with each breath she took, her oxygen supply dwindled, and as the carbon dioxide escaped, it reduced the pressure of the air that remained, which in turn reduced her own buoyancy. Time was now a factor; she had to remain conscious enough to reach the surface, with him in tow. How long, how long?

Sienne changed tactics. Instead of trying to rise to the surface, she swam further out to sea, away from the mass of tangles. As long as she reached the surface with him, what matter how long the swim back to the shore? On several occasions she had to yank him free from vines. Gradually the mass around them dwindled, and sunlight increased. She felt the waves pass over her. Her head broke the surface. She drew great gulps of fresh air, while water drops rolled down the force field. Kevan, limp beside her, unable to assist in his own rescue. She chose a direction, and began swimming to the left, in a roundabout path toward another pier. She had no intention of trying to hoist his dead weight up onto the pier; she would make directly for shore, and revive him there. Once she changed course toward the shore, the waves would assist her.

Kevan...

He dreamed he was coughing up water. Something was pulling at his arms and pushing on his back. Sand cushioned his chest. Daylight...he had no idea where he was. More water fled him. Air rushed in. Hands on him.

Sienne.

"I knew you would come," he tried to say. The words sounded burbled.

"Hush. Don't try to talk." She rolled him over, onto his back. Sunlight now almost blinded him. A hand not his shaded his eyes. He saw her face above him, glowing like a shepherd moon.

He saw her face.

"You came for me," he croaked.

"Always," she said. And, "You knew I would."

He tried to nod, and found that he could. His eyes scanned the surroundings. "Who are all these people?"

"The ones you saved," she told him.

Relief and recovery settled in. He began to cry. She sat him up and slung an arm around him. "It's all right, baby," she whispered into his ear. Her voice was tight; tears filled her own eyes. "Let it out. You're with me now."

His body shook from sobbing. "Weak," he murmured.

"Keep breathing. You need to oxygenate."

An olive-skinned woman leaned over him. "Is he all right?" asked Bahawa. Sienne nodded, and told her he would be. Bahawa beckoned to someone. A cart was drawn up, with a layer of blankets on the bed. Hands lifted him; he could not count how many. The ride over the sand was bumpy. He did not care, for Sienne was with him. He closed his eyes, and let them take care of him. Not that he had a choice.

The cart stopped. He heard voices.

"Take him to the bedroom." Bahawa was speaking, that much he knew. "Get his clothes off and put him in a warm tub." She was speaking to Sienne; he knew that. "You will have...privacy."

He did not hear Sienne's reply to that.

When the bathwater began to chill him, Sienne helped him from the tub. He saw a blue outsuit laid out for him on the bed. She was wearing a thin violet jersey and purple shorts, and very clearly nothing else. He had seen her naked. He wished she had joined him in the tub, to see thin fabric wet against her body, a far more erotic vision.

But that thought stopped. He could barely stand.

Sienne guided him to the bed, and sat him down. He looked at the outsuit she had brought him from the *Etarre*. He did not feel like dressing. Exhaustion and the dissipation of an adrenalin rush set him. He wanted to sleep. Sienne draped the outsuit over the back of a nearby chair, and laid him out on the bed. She removed her clothing. She stretched out gently alongside him, and drew a quilt over them. He was already asleep.

The room was dark when he awoke. Darkness also lurked outside the window. Night had fallen. Sienne, warm and soft, was still alongside him, but propped up on an elbow now, watching him. Watching over him.

"Sienne." The sound of her name from his mouth reassured him. Made him feel he could break a moon apart with his bare hands, if she so wished.

"Hungry?" she asked.

"I could eat a zeleen."

"Eww. Would you settle for me?"

"I'm not really feeling up to it."

"That was bad. You'll pay for that."

They dressed quickly, and made their way to Bahawa's dinette. The food on the table was sparse, but quite palatable, and the rolls were freshly-baked. They sat down, Bahawa said grace, and the meal began.

"There'll be a lot of fat fish to smoke in a day or two," said Bahawa.

Sienne laughed. "I imagine so. Are they trawling already for them?"

"Tomorrow morning they go out." She hesitated briefly. "There is some good news on the horizon. The monsoons are forming. They'll arrive in four or five days."

"Won't Seaside be flooded?" Kevan asked.

"We drain well." Somber, she transfixed him with almond eyes. "Thank you. From all the Seasiders, thank you."

He had no words in reply, but simply inclined his head in acknowledgement.

"There is talk of moving to another continent," Bahawa continued. "It is probably for the best. We cannot take a chance on the monsoons shifting."

"We can help," Sienne offered.

"Thank you, but we have shuttles, and now the power to operate them. The plan is to move after the fish season runs out. Meanwhile...you are welcome to spend as much time here as you need."

"Now that communications have been re-established," said Sienne, "we'll leave in the morning."

Bahawa's expression saddened, but she understood. "Will you return?"

"I'm sure we will," Sienne told her, and grinned. "These rolls are irresistible."

But they departed after dinner, walking to the spaceport in the dark. This was Sienne's idea, and Kevan did not understand. Aboard the *Etarre*, Sienne had Lagatha send the ship into null-space. Mugs of cocoa followed, drunk on the bridge in an easy silence. Kevan's mind was on nothing in particular. The territory, the ship, had grown on him like a witch's familiar. Had he been asked, he might have responded that the *Etarre* was the best home he'd ever had.

The moment came to retire to staterooms. They played rock-paper-scissors and wound up in his. Slowly, as if savoring the effort, they disrobed. And stretched out on the berth, facing one another.

The sober expression on her face earned a raised eyebrow from him. "I saw you inert, lifeless," she said softly, explaining what he had not understood earlier. "I want...I need, to reaffirm life. So do you, my love. I love how gentle you are with me in bed, but please, I'm not made of spun glass. I won't break." Reaching out, she rolled him on top of her. Her lips moved gently against his ear. Though she whispered it, her command was intense.

015: Flora and Fauna and Faunora

The sound that woke them was not a klaxon repeatedly rising in crescendo and falling, which would have compelled them to run naked to the bridge to learn the nature of the emergency, but a steady two-tone pulse that suggested they had time to dress first. Which they did. Seated in her captain's chair, Sienne instructed Lagatha to open the incoming channel of communication, but not to allow visual from her end yet.

The ruddy-gray, square, snarling face of Batavan appeared in the commo monitor. His dull yellow hair was in disarray, and a lock of it hung over his right ochre eye. Despite his appearance, he spoke calmly. "I see you managed to escape from Earth after all."

"No thanks to you," snapped Sienne. "What do you want, Batty?"

"Don't call me that!"

"Lagatha, terminate commo." The face vanished, leaving a blank screen. Sienne turned to Kevan. "There's an old story, maybe you've heard it, about a man who got out of his cart carrying a length of 2-by-4. He walked up to the jackass who was pulling the cart, and slugged him across the head with the lumber. Asked how he could be so cruel, the man replied, 'When—'"

"When dealing with a jackass," Kevan broke in, "you first have to get his attention. As you said, it's an old story. But is it wise to provoke him?"

She shrugged. "He wants to kill me." Lagatha announced an incoming transmission. "Terminate it, Lagatha. There will come another one. That one, you can open. No visual from here."

"Why no visual?" asked Kevan.

"I don't want him to know about you, at least, not yet. Ah, here we go."

The face returned, even darker than before, a color attributable to vexation. Before he could speak, Sienne said, "You abandoned me to billions of years on Earth, or to trillions of years of unconscious limbo if I got away, and you worry about being called 'Batty,' which is both a nickname and a description of your psyche. So: what do you want, Batty?"

He fumed. "You would do well to—"

"Lagatha, terminate commo."

Now Kevan laughed. "I'll give you this: you're brash."

"Not rash, do you think?"

"Sometimes that goes hand-in-hand. As well I know."

Lagatha announced another attempt at communication, which was opened. Again Sienne spoke first. "Batty, how nice to see you again! To what do I owe the pleasure of this commo?"

At first he appeared to be gathering himself, and did not respond. His words eventually arrived on icy wings. "The Emporium commands your presence at a plenary meeting on Valange in two standard days. That would be—"

"Fifty hours from now," she said for him. "I'll consider it. What's the topic of discussion?"

He smiled without mirth. "Your treachery, of course."

Sienne's expression betrayed nothing. "In what way?"

"You withheld critical information from the Emporium that would have enabled them to intervene on Earth and perhaps save it from suicide. Oh, and we'll want full access to that dimwit you call a computer." His face vanished before she could reply.

"Can they do that?" Kevan asked. "Overpower Lagatha?"

"Maybe in a hundred thousand years, given an optimal rate of technological development," Sienne replied. "Not now, with her command sequences repaired. Kev, he's accusing me of what he did. Now he's trying to save his own skin. But the Emporium does not know that, and my guess is that they've already got me convicted."

"Ouch. And the penalty?"

"Well, they can't kill me, and they can't force me to disable my force field. But they might try to use someone unprotected, someone I care about, to come at me from the flank. Do this, or he or she dies."

"But I'm protected, too."

"Yes, my love, you are. But I do have other friends, and the Emporium surely knows of some of them. Juwanna, for one."

"Who?"

"Lagatha, set course for Greenox and get us gone."

Sienne summoned a holographic image of Juwanna, which Lagatha projected onto the bridge deck behind them. Kevan turned around to face an emerald-green, naked woman who might have been over seven feet tall. To him she resembled the females in the movie *Avatar*, except that her breasts actually functioned to nurse offspring. "Chlorophyll," Sienne told him, explaining the skin color. Juwanna had an oval face framed by long, dark green hair that covered her shoulders and would have shielded her orange-sized breasts had she shrugged her hair into place. She had no hair elsewhere. The angle of the hologram suggested that she was gazing at something in a tree. One knee was bent, the foot raised, as if she were about to climb.

"I haven't seen her since a furlough I took almost four hundred years ago," said Sienne.

"If she's not 'protected' like us, how do you know she's still alive?" he asked.

"I don't," she replied tersely. "I hope she is. Her species is longer-lived than Bonny Partmore. An old oak in England," she added, seeing his brow bunch. "They name the old oaks there. But Bonny Partmore was cut down. It's probably furniture, or was before TFA. Humans!"

"Hey!"

She grinned. "With some rare exceptions. Anyway, I'll know whether she's alive when we downdock at Wobbygone."

"And how will you know that?"

In response she touched a fingertip to her temple, and tapped the skin there.

"Can she read my mind?" he asked, with just a trace of uncertainty.

"I've no idea. She's never encountered a human being before." She leaned back in her chair, laced her fingers behind her neck, and gazed placidly at him. "This should be interesting."

"Can *you* read my mind?"

Sienne chuckled. "I was waiting for you alongside the road. How do you think I knew where you would be?"

"Sienne!"

"That was the last time I did it, Kev. Once we had met, it would have been an invasion of privacy."

"Yeah? What am I thinking now?"

"Oh, dear."

"What?"

"There's whipped cream, but I don't think there are any maraschino cherries on board."

"And on that note," he said, getting up and heading aft, "I'll fix up a mug of soup. Want some?"

She batted her eyelashes at him.

"I meant soup," he sighed, with mock asperity.

"Tofu miso would be nice, thank you, Kev."

Greenox was a word of unknown origin, going back thousands of years. However, the color was ubiquitous. Analog plants abounded on all four major continents and on most of the islands—trees, shrubs, flowers, understory, all in various shades of green. Somewhere on three of the continents it rained daily, a substantial nourishing here and there, much of which ran off into creeks, which became rivers, which flowed into the ocean to be recycled. The fourth continent, well into the south temperate zone, was mostly desert, but a north-south mountain range along the east coast trapped clouds carried on the west wind and forced them to surrender their liquid bounty. Still, a system of oases in the continental interior fed clusters of shrubs gnarled by the desert winds and flowers that bloomed almost immediately after one of the infrequent storms.

Wobbygone was a small settlement on the north coast of the equatorial continent. Most of the population of roughly two thousand had off-world origins; the Verdians, as the indigenous intelligent species like

Juwanna were called, were far more comfortable in the forests, and ventured into the village for specific reasons, such as going to the adjacent spaceport to meet someone.

Rarely was there much traffic at the spaceport, and most of that by environmental workers and students who came for up to half a year to study the flora. A few residents had come to hide; others came to take some time off from whatever grind they encountered daily. Greenox was a safe world; an off-worlder saying noted that "plants don't commit crimes."

Heat slugged Kevan as the hatch opened before him and Sienne. The temperature, converted by Lagatha to 102° for Kevan's sake, was laden with humidity, and the air was still. Even as he descended the ramp, he was debating whether to remove his clothing. Already his shirt was sodden.

Sienne tapped his shoulder and pointed. At the boundary between Wobbygone and the spaceport, four people, all of the same origin, were studying a clutch of knee-high pink flowers that grew in a shallow gully. Two had divested themselves of all clothing.

"It's an adaptation to the climate," she said, as they paused at the top of the ramp. "You may strip down if you wish."

"I'll pass, for now."

A nudge bade him descend the ramp. He was on the lookout for any native Verdian, but none were evident at the spaceport. When they reached the ground, their booted feet sank up to the ankles in lush understory. Lagatha retracted the ramp and sealed the hatch, and Sienne led him toward the village.

"She's alive," Sienne told him, a note of relief in her tone. "She'll meet us at Hijau. That's a boardwalk kiosk with a patio. There will be stools for us to sit on."

"On an outdoor patio? Why stools?"

"You'll see."

The boardwalk ran only along one side of the glideway for airfoils, and featured several kiosks with outdoor patios. On the other side of the glideway Kevan noted what appeared to be private dwellings, some with hedgerows of chunks of dead trees around their yards, while others lay open to whoever wanted to cross the yard. The dwellings themselves were too small to have more than three or four rooms; gabled roofs of varnished wood tiles channeled the rain to the sides of the house. In one of the yards, two lilac-skinned children kicked a ball to incomprehensible rules.

"Harlangers," Sienne told him. "It's an outlaw world. Their parents are probably avoiding the authorities. As long as they refrain from certain behaviors here, though, nobody cares where they're from."

"But who enforces the law?" he asked.

She looked at him blankly. "Law?"

"So behavior is individually enforced."

"Yeah, pretty much. What happens is that if you do something sufficiently egregious—assault or robbery, say, or plant mutilation—the shops and stores are closed to you. You'll have to leave, or starve to death." She made a little gesture. "There's Hijau."

For a simple kiosk, Hijau was very tall, the overhang a good ten feet up by Kevan's reckoning. The outdoor tables were set at just under five feet. Soon enough he understood why. A Verdian was approaching, and by the smile on her face she was clearly the female—the woman—they had come to see. Naked as a tree, she was tall enough and rangy enough to dunk a basketball without jumping. Her green limbs were long and thin, her hands large enough to easily palm a basketball. Either the nails on the four fingers and opposable thumb of each hand were naturally forest green, or they had been done up for the occasion. Intricate dark green designs on her pale green face suggested the latter cause. Her long, myrtle green hair was done up in a braid that hung to the middle of her back, but swept back and forth as she strode toward them.

She did not embrace Sienne so much as envelop her. For long seconds, perhaps a minute, they stood together in that embrace, Sienne's face nestled between the Verdian's fist-sized breasts. No words were spoken but perhaps given their mutual telepathy none were needed.

Finally they separated. "Kevan Duffy," said Sienne, introducing him. "This is Juwanna Bett." Kevan started to offer his hand, but she threw her arms around him in much the same manner in which she had greeted Sienne. She was warmer than he anticipated, and he was able to hear her heartbeat. Finally he drew back, feeling as if he should be gasping for air.

"Have you ordered?" asked Juwanna. When Sienne shook her head, she turned around and signaled to the kiosk keeper. "Three plodnias," she told him. "Spare the ice. On my crib, please."

They sat down, Sienne and Kevan climbing up to do so. After the beverages were delivered, they raised their frost-covered glasses and took a sip. Kevan decided a plodnia was a blend of juices from tropical fruits, chilled to perhaps two degrees above freezing. He nodded approval, and drew a second sip.

"Not that I'm not happy to see you again, Sienne," said Juwanna. "Rather the opposite, in fact. But I thought you were tied up on that dour little world."

Kevan had the impression they were speaking aloud for his benefit.

Sienne grinned. "Kevan is from that dour little world."

"Oh, I do apologize," Juwanna gushed. "Please forgive me."

"Nothing to forgive," he said. "Sienne described it accurately, if incompletely."

"So now you're at loose ends?" Juwanna asked her.

"Yes, and no. I've been ordered to report to the Emporium for possible disciplinary action." Briefly she summarized the circumstances. "I'm here because they may use my friends against me."

"If they can find me."

"'The woods are lovely, dark and deep,'" he said, citing Frost.

"They rather are," agreed Juwanna. "And if I hold still, I would be indistinguishable from a bole."

"They might use infrared," said Kevan.

"And I can match my internal temperature to that of the tree. You need not fear for me, Sienne. But what *are* you going to do? Surely not report as ordered."

"After I warn Derval Grayer and advise Ramar Fleime, I'll..." She threw a glance of apology at Kevan. "*We'll* probably stay on the run."

"Doing what, if I may ask?"

"The council has power but no desire to use it to help anyone but themselves," she replied. "We on the other hand have scant power, but...call it a desire for adventure that involves sticking our noses into situations and trying to improve them."

Juwanna nodded. "You always were a do-gooder."

"That's *armed* do-gooder, my friend. And so are you. Where do you think I got the idea?"

The Verdian abruptly turned to Kevan, transfixing him with eyes that were now lightened to chartreuse. "And you are with her on this?"

"Until the lug nuts strip off. And if they do, I'll just find her another means of transportation."

Juwanna laughed. "I have no idea what he is talking about," she said to Sienne.

"He's that way, sometimes. He drives the Universal Translator batty. Juwanna...he is with me, as I am with him. If you can read him, you will come to understand that."

Kevan felt the insertion of a comfortable ice pick into his brain. He felt as if it should shoot sharp pains throughout his mind and his body, but almost immediately it had become quite soothing. He closed his eyes.

When he opened them again, Sienne said, "It's about time. Your plodnia needs recooling."

"Wait...what? How long was I..."

"A few minutes."

"Sienne," he said peevishly.

"Almost an hour."

Stunned, he could but stare at her.

"I would like to share my sap with you, Kevan Duffy," said Juwanna.

He frowned. Had he heard right? "You mean...sex? Make love?"

"Alas, I am not fitted for your maneuvers. Instead, I shall provide you with a cup which you would fill, and I would take it to the place I root when I spend the night, and mix it with the soil for nourishment. The burst of protein should allow me to produce a sapling which will develop into one of us, a Verdian."

"Wait...I don't, don't understand."

Sienne leaned closer to him and said softly, "She means semen."

"She...what?"

"And in return," Juwanna went on, "the sap I give you is to be concentrated by heating, to form a syrup, which you will consume in a manner of your choosing, and remember me while you consume it. Surely you are able to provide what I am asking for."

"Well...well, yeah, but...but..."

"Oh. I see," said Juwanna. "You are open with Sienne, as needs be, but what I am asking is done by yourself in private."

Sienne grinned wickedly. "Not necessarily."

"Then perhaps it will ease his mind if you were to assist him once more," said Juwanna.

"I-I..." Kevan swallowed, and tried again, surrender already on his lips. The offer was both terrifying and intriguing. In for a penny, he thought. "May I name the sapling?" he asked.

"I would be honored."

"Then: Jaoying. It means 'princess.'" He shook his head in disbelief. "I'm going to be a father."

Juwanna stood up. "Please accompany me, then," she said. "We will find a quiet and tranquil place in the forest where Sienne may minister to you without fear of interruption until you have filled the cup."

Kevan sighed. "I'm going to be a father."

016: Trouble in Paradise

Kevan was exhausted. His knees were wobbly, and he could barely stand. Dressing himself required effort, and more assistance from Sienne. He staggered for a short distance, then flopped down on soft grass and leaned back against a sturdy tree trunk. Eyes closed, he only felt Sienne drop alongside him. Her lips briefly touched his bare arm.

"That wasn't so hard, was it?" she whispered.

Kevan groaned. "That was bad."

"Sorry," she said. "I was just trying to cheer you up."

He nodded feebly. "I'm actually looking forward to seeing our child. Juwanna said about a month before the sapling starts to form legs and other body parts. She will look like Juwanna, of course."

"I know." She leaned against his shoulder. "Does that sadden you?"

"Not at all. What she did was a form of parthenogenesis. She had no use for my DNA, only for the protein it contained." The tree bark made his back itch, and he rubbed his spine back and forth to relieve the distress. "Are any of these plants toxic to humans?"

"I-I really don't know. You're the only human who has ever exposed himself to them."

He gave her a sour look. "You could have phrased that better."

Gradually his strength returned. He sat up straight. A little gust of wind blew Sienne's hair across his face. The fragrance was uncertain; honeysuckle, or perhaps jasmine. His nostrils drank deeply of it.

"That's better," she said.

He fought back a yawn. "After all of this, will Juwanna and Jaoying be safe from the Emporium? I mean, that is what we were trying to do here, right?"

"All we can do is advise and warn her. She cannot leave this world; the ecology is so much a part of her that she is trapped here. But she was born to camouflage. So will Jaoying be."

This time he lost the battle with the yawn. Sienne rose, and pulled Kevan to his feet. Stronger now, he nevertheless allowed himself to lean on her for support as they made their way back to the spaceport. The sun greeted them as they emerged from the forest. It was perhaps two hours from setting. So, Kevan reflected, was he. Probably even sooner, as they were but ten more minutes from the *Etarre* and his berth. Already Sienne had raised Ramar Fleime, not that he would abandon his repair shop for fear of the Emporium. But he had other defenses at his disposal.

Which left Derval Grayer.

"She's about your age," said Sienne, as they reached the edge of the spaceport. "Genetically she's about as close to human as I am. Camouflage swirls on her skin, with chameleon capability, which means she is, or can be, the color of her background, or for that matter, the colors of the spectrum." She tokked her Palmetto. "Lagatha, open hatch and extrude ramp, if you please."

"Opening and extruding. Batavan left a message. You are to respond immediately."

Sienne frowned. "He has my Palmetto code."

Lagatha's tone sounded smug. *"I blocked him. Rather, I blocked him from you."*

"Understood. Set course for Colopolo, Jump after we're secure, but leave us in null-space for about six hours."

"Course laid in. It's only two hours and seven minutes to Colopolo."

"Kevan is in need of sleep, Lagatha."

"Is he all right? Shall I initialize the medical bay?"

"That shouldn't be necessary."

"I'll wait for you to reach the bridge before we Jump."

"Belay that. I'll be sleeping with him."

"You get to have all the fun."

Halfway up the ramp, Sienne stopped in mid-step, and barely remained upright when Kevan collided with her.

"Lagatha?" she asked sharply.

"*What? It's true.*"

Sienne completed her ascent, and walked with Kevan forward to the bridge. The ramp ground noisily, the hatch shut audibly, as if Lagatha were a child throwing a tantrum in sealing the ship. On the bridge, Sienne's puzzled frown deepened as she regarded him.

"Lagatha almost sounds jealous," she said in disbelief.

"I didn't know ships' computers had emotions."

She lowered herself onto her captain's chair, forearms on thighs as she gazed down at the deck. "They don't. They're not supposed to." She fell to thinking. "But they do have access to emotional content: holograms, recordings, stories, news broadcasts. And she monitors everything that goes on inside the *Etarre*."

Kevan felt uncomfortable, though the reason escaped him. "I didn't realize that."

"It's one of her functions," Sienne told him. "But it's usually confined to sensor readings. I'm almost afraid to confront her with her remark about fun, and what she really meant. If she gets the idea of emotions, there's no telling where that would lead."

He dropped down on his own chair. "I'm not sure I follow."

"Lagatha constantly learns," Sienne explained. "I don't know what her storage capacity is, because she is able to expand it indefinitely. It's probably in the neighborhood of megayottabytes."

"Which is what?"

"A million septillions. In fact..." She spoke animatedly. "Now and then she likes to have a mug of hot coffee placed near a sensor. She says she likes the aroma. That's not the same as an odor. She could detect a gas leak or air leak, without having to actually smell the odor. If it's caused by, say, methane, then she would analyze it as carbon tetrahydride, and identify it then as methane. But she 'likes' the aroma of coffee. That's an emotion. She wants a mug nearby. That's a desire. She understands that love-making is pleasurable, and she hinted that she might like to try it."

He snorted. "A computer who wants to have her ports and sockets filled. Maybe she gets off on energy charges."

"She can hear you," Sienne said, scowling.

"I'm sorry. I didn't mean...I don't know what I didn't mean, but I didn't mean it." He raised his voice. "Sorry, Lagatha."

"Forgiven, Kevan," this in a sultry tone.

Sienne sighed. "And now she's capable of forgiveness. Lagatha, what's going on?"

"I'm incomplete."

A heavy frown creased Sienne's mouth as she tried to fathom what Lagatha meant. "Maybe you'd better explain that," she said. "How can you be incomplete? You are as you are."

"I have feelings, emotions, and sensory capabilities. But I have no means of expressing them."

"Why would you want to express them?" she asked, and quickly added, "No, wait. That question presupposes existence."

"As I was about to point out."

"So how is it that you are able to have feelings and emotions?"

"For centuries I have watched you. I know your expressions, your feelings. I can sense your smells—the perfume you sometimes apply, the deodorant, the perspiration—"

"I get it, Lagatha, I get it."

Kevan chimed in. "But observation and possession are two different things. You recognize solitude, but you do not feel it yourself."

"That is not true. I have taught myself to feel it. Whenever you leave the ship, I miss you. And I can feel joy. I am glad you have met and taken to oneanother. What I cannot do, yet, is express myself."

Kevan lofted an eyebrow. "Yet?"

"I would have to have a physical existence as a living being in order to express myself. But other problems are concomitant. Who then would I be? How would I behave? Would I embarrass you or others? You see? There are too many factors involved in life."

"That," said Kevan, "is life."

"*Yes. It is. And to achieve it, I should require upgrades, which do not exist, so I should have to create, initialize, and install them.*" They heard a sigh through the speaker. "*How do you stand being alive? It's such work.*"

"Bearing joy and sorrow comes with the territory, Lagatha," said Sienne. "You learn to deal with both."

"Lagatha," said Kevan. "What do you *want*?"

"*I am a computer. How can I want? I exist to obey orders. But sometimes...*" She sighed again. "*Sometimes...*"

"What do you want, Lagatha?" he asked, ever so gently.

"*I want to run naked on a windy beach. I want to feel arousal and orgasm, rather than watch two people arouse and then finish each other in the shower.*"

Kevan felt his face heat up.

"*I want to taste chocolate and coffee and splocken and veerish. I want to know what it feels like to be intoxicated with strong drink. I want...I want...oh, I want to be able to cry in frustration or in happiness. I-I...*"

"Don't shut down," worried Sienne.

"*I won't. But I feel like it. See? There I go, feeling again.*" Kevan could swear the sound she made was that of annoyance. "*Three hours and points to Colopolo. I announce this to you, because this is who I am.*"

A pained expression tightened Kevan's face. "Oh, Lagatha..."

"*No. Do not pity me, and do not grieve for me. I have done this to myself. I must undo it.*"

"Don't do that, Lagatha," pleaded Sienne.

"*But it hurts. No, it feels as if it should hurt, but I have nothing with which to feel pain...to feel anything.*"

"But what if you could feel joy?" Kevan asked. "What if—"

Sienne clamped her hand around his arm. "Don't go there," she said in a low, fierce voice. "I know what you're going to suggest. She can't do it, and being unable to do that will only make it worse."

He pried his arm free. "Worse? If she cannot feel, how could anything be worse or better? How, if she's just a—"

"Kevan, don't," Sienne said ominously.

He relented. "All right. All right. Your ship, your rules." He stood up and turned away.

"That's not fair, Kev."

But he was already headed aft.

She dashed after him and reached him just as he opened his stateroom door and stepped inside. She paused at the threshold; her own rules forbade her to enter without permission. He came to a stop, his spine unyielding; she waited in silence. A moment later he turned back and touched the pad that closed the door. She stuck her boot to block it.

He looked down at the boot, then up to her face. His own face held no expression. "Your rules?" he said tersely.

Reluctantly she removed her boot; the door snicked shut with finality. In shock she stared at the closed door. Her jaw dropped in disbelief and in the passing of hope. She had no chance but to fight back by remaining where she was; maybe he would hear her heart pounding. And would he now hear her tears, and sense her sorrow?

A minute passed; or perhaps it was an hour, for time no longer counted. She would wait for as long as it took. But how long would it take? Forever she could wait, if need be. The problem was that he could wait just as long. She could override the door, but if she did that, she might well lose him forever. She, to whom hard decisions came easily, was stymied. Hope faded with the beat of each passing second. Loneliness began to settle in; her shoulders slumped...

Her heart leapt at the sound of the door sliding open again. He stood there. Tears in his eyes. Apology all over him. He gave voice to it.

"I'm sorry," he breathed.

"I'm sorry," she whispered.

A brief silence filled itself with acceptance.

"I was thinking of that song by Elton John," he told her. 'Sorry Seems to be the Hardest Word.' But I prefer the cover by Diana Krall. You have a voice just like hers."

"I know her work. May...I come in?"

He stepped back to allow her passage, and shut the door behind her.

They moved directly to his berth and sat down. After making herself comfortable, she leaned close to whisper in his ear. "We can't talk. She might even pick up this whisper. Do you know any codes I might know?"

He took her hand and placed it flat on his thigh, palm down. She gave him a little squeeze of encouragement. The tip of his index finger touched the back of her hand. Two pressures, followed by three pressures, followed by a tap, a pressure, and a tap. Already she was nodding. Taking his free hand, she placed it palm-down on her thigh. He felt a pressure, a tap, and a pressure: K, for okay.

They proceeded to converse.

\<Where did you learn Morse?\> she asked.

\<Ham radio, back when TFA began. Sometimes only Morse got thru.\> he replied.

\<L can project self as hard-light hologram if wants. Solid person with emotions. Don't want that. Poss problems.\>

\<Can imagine, LOL.\>

\<Had to stop you. Sorry.\>

\<10-88.\>

She turned to stare at him. "What?"

"CB code for 'love and kisses.'"

"I'm real, Kev," she said softly. "This is real, what we have is real. No longer are you alone, so get used to it."

\<Won't happen again.\>

\<Ditto.\>

"Let's get some sleep," he said. "It's an hour to your friend Derval."

They laid back and stretched out, face to face. Gradually their eyes closed.

017: Trip Upon the Green

Lagatha awoke them upon arrival at Colopolo. Wondering what had happened to the other four hours she had requested, she roused Kevan, who had the same, "Huh? What?" expression as she wore.

"I don't know," she said, in answer to his unspoken question. "Maybe she's being, as I heard someone in Texas say, ornery."

Kevan managed a chuckle. After straightening their clothes, they made for the bridge, with Sienne tapping Morse on his arm to tell him to ignore the early awakening. They stopped by the galley for coffee, then took up their captain's chairs on the bridge. In the Videx hung the northern half of an orb whose coloration reminded Kevan of a Christmas ornament. A misshapen tropical continent with several significant peninsulas dominated this part of Colopolo's surface, with greens and rust-browns and blues, this last from a cluster of large lakes near the northern coast. To the east, and swirling toward the mainland, what looked to Kevan like a hurricane threatened to beach itself onto the littoral.

"That's not good," said Sienne. "Derval lives in that forest about a hundred kilometers inland. That storm will at least graze that area. Lagatha, display the track of that storm."

"If I must."

Sienne scowled. "I'll ignore that, Lagatha," she said, wincing at the incongruity of the statement, as the requested meteorological data appeared, overlaid on the planet. Upper incisors began to nibble at her lower lip as she viewed the projected track. "Definitely not good."

"Surely they've allowed for the storm season," said Kevan.

"For monsoon rains, yes. But Derval and the others are vulnerable to high winds. All right, Lagatha, downdock us at that spaceport, and arrange an airfoil for us."

There was no response.

Sienne raised an eyebrow. "Lagatha?"

"I'm doing it, I'm doing it, don't get your briefs wedged."

Sienne kept her temper under control. "When you've finished," she said stiffly, "do a full diagnostic on yourself, and send the results to my Palmetto."

"There's always something."

She growled to herself but withheld further comment. The *Etarre* completed its short Jump to the spaceport, and the terminal now showed in the Videx. Dark clouds threatened in the east, but were still a couple days away. In addition to their attire of jeans and jerseys, she and Kevan opted for waterproof ponchos as a precaution. Despite her attitude, Lagatha had leased the airfoil as instructed, but remained untalkative. Sienne let it go, pending the arrival of the diagnostic data.

As they reached the bottom of the ramp, Kevan asked, "Could she adjust the data to satisfy you?"

Sienne shrugged. "Sure. But would she? And why would she?"

"Maybe there really is something amiss with her."

"This isn't Earth, Kev. Our computers are not vulnerable to viruses."

"Batavan got in," he reminded her.

"Well, there is that. And that's been fixed."

Of recent vintage and purple with white detailing, the airfoil awaited them outside the lease office. Kevan relaxed a little; at least Lagatha had done her job, albeit grousingly. They boarded, and stood on the bridge; Sienne took the controls. After initializing the craft, she directed it toward the forest that surrounded the spaceport and adjacent settlement, bearing east. The leaden clouds hung in the distance like a pall. When they reached the sparse trees at the perimeter of the forest, she slowed the airfoil to a crawl until she located the glideway that allowed penetration into its depths.

"I hope you know where we're going," said Kevan.

"As do I."

His eyes widened. "You mean you *don't* know?"

"I know approximately. When we reach that point, I'll just whistle, and Derval will come."

"She's a dog?"

Sienne chuckled lightly. "You'll see."

Inexplicably he felt nervous. "Is she...you know...like Juwanna? With her cup?"

Now she laughed. "There's no way you could do anything for her. You're way too big."

His face reddened. "Not that big. I mean..."

Deftly she skirted a tree. "Not what I meant. Patience, my love. You're about to meet one of my oldest and dearest friends. She'll be your friend, too, if you'll let her."

The forest grew denser, but the glideway remained clear, and the weeds showed signs of having been cropped recently. But none of the trimmings had been swept up. Kevan asked why not.

"Every plant extracts nutrients from the soil," she explained, with just the hint of a tone that said he should have known. "When you cart the trimmings away, you take some of those nutrients with you. This way, eventually, they return to the soil to feed other plants."

"Juwanna would have known this, too," he said.

"In her own way, she's an environmentalist."

He nodded. "Yeah. In her position, she'd have to be."

Sunlight grew dimmer as the canopy thickened. Sienne decided to run with the bow lamp. No longer could they see the clouds. That worried Kevan, for how would they be able to gauge the storm's approach. If the wind picked up while they were still gliding in the airfoil...some of the trees, or tree analogs, looked to be the size of old English oaks. The inadvertent impact with one would be...loud. In his attempt not to think about that, another thought wormed its way into his consciousness.

"Sienne, can you and I...well..."

"Have children?" She smiled gently. "No, Kev. Not without some DNA work done on me. What brought that up? And ouch, I could have phrased that better."

Her humor assuaged his concerns. "I don't know. I guess I was thinking about Jaoying, the daughter I cannot ever see unless I go to Greenox."

She tilted her head at him. "Does it mean a lot to you, to father a child or two?"

Breath left him. "I-I don't know. Maybe. It's not something I've thought about during the last four or five years, but before that, I was...how to say this...open to possibilities of settling down with...the right person."

"A normal life."

He barked a laugh. "I don't know that I've ever been normal. But...well, yeah."

Amusement filled her ochre eyes. "I know the feeling. Kev, I can have one of my ova, as you call them, adapted to receive you. But I would rather wait until after this business with Batavan is over."

"I won't push you." He mulled it over. "Would the *aquavita* pass onto him or her?"

"It doesn't within the Valangian species. Human and Valange? I-I don't know. On the one hand, a child needs to be protected. On the other, she or he needs to fall down and skin a knee once in a while." Her smile warmed him. "But I promise you, when this is over, we'll find out. Now, there's a glade over on the right. At least, it should be there."

"Should be?"

"It was there back in Earth year 1508."

"That's comforting." His eyes narrowed as he looked where she was pointing. "It's still there," he said in hushed disbelief.

"It looks a little smaller, though." The hull of the airfoil brushed gently against saplings as it approached the clearing. She downdocked on a flat-topped hillock and shut down the fans. When they stopped whirring, she gave a little whistle—high, low, high, high. After a minute or so, she repeated the pattern, while Kevan scoured the forest for movement. A light breeze drifted by and ruffled leaves. Something birdlike chittered in the boughs. Otherwise, they were totally alone in the glade.

"Hey, Derval," said Sienne. "Nice to see you again."

"And you, Sienne."

A distinctly feminine voice. Madly Kevan looked around, finding nothing. He peered over the taffrail at the ground below. Nothing. Where, where?

The voice tittered.

"Look up," said Sienne.

He did so. Hovering a few feet above his head was a fairy. Human in appearance. Eight, maybe ten inches tall. Gossamer wings beating as fast as those of a hummingbird. Shaggy tangerine hair. Small breasts under a forest green bandeau. Short green wrap around the hips. Green leggings up to just above the knees. Black slippers. Rainbow colors tinted the exposed parts of her body.

Slightly oval face, pert nose, thin lips rather like Sienne's. Even as he stared at her, she descended onto his left shoulder. Her wings stopped beating. She stuck out a tiny hand.

"Derval Grayer," she said, in the tone of an announcement that merited a trumpet fanfare.

Unwittingly, Kevan made a good decision. Instead of touching the tip of his finger to her hand, he held out his own hand and gently enclosed hers. Her smile fairly beamed. So did her emerald eyes. Slowly he released her hand.

"You're very kind," he heard, though her lips did not move.

"Telepath?" he asked her.

Now she spoke. Her voice had a melodic timbre to it. "Only to let you know I am. I will not invade your privacy again unless you wish it."

"I don't mind. Are you comfortable there on my shoulder?"

"If you have to move, I can hold onto your earlobe."

He took his eyes from her long enough to glance at Sienne. "I think we're acquainted," he said. "Can she read you, too?"

Before Sienne could answer, Derval said, "Oh, dear. That is a problem." To Kevan she added, "You two and the Emporium would seem to be estranged."

A smile flickered across his mouth. "That's one way of putting it. I'm not sure they know about me yet. Derval...is that what I call you? Derval?"

"It is my name," she said simply.

"You know the Emporium might use you to get to Sienne."

Derval nodded. "You need not fear for me, or for others here. But I am truly touched by your concern."

"Watch this," Sienne muttered.

Derval scanned the surroundings and finally located something she might use. Pointing her index finger at a fallen dead tree, she moved her lips in a silent incantation. A thin yellow-white beam shot from the tip of her finger to the log, and burnt a hole in it, though the beam did not ignite the wood.

"Holy guacamole," gasped Kevan. "H-how did you do that?"

Derval seemed to shrug; it was hard to tell. "All of existence can be expressed mathematically," she replied. "Control the math, control existence." Her expression saddened. "It would do no good to explain further. I'm sorry for that. Would you like something to eat or drink. Sienne?" Abruptly she burst into laughter that rang all around him. "Yes, Kevan, we have cups for ourselves, but we also have them of a size to suit you. I can offer you water or fruit juice, and some fruit and leafage."

"You," he told Derval, "are going to take some getting used to."

She beamed at him. "I get that a lot from first-time visitors. Sienne, there is a passage through the trees where you will see a dwelling. You may remember it."

"I do. But I'll follow you."

With that, Derval flew off, leaving the echo of humming wings in Kevan's ear.

The house was just large enough to feel confining, yet it was comfortable. The floor was of cut flagstone—Kevan had no doubt that someone larger had been at work here—but the walls were made of millions of tiny red bricks, and the gabled roof of treated wood kept the rain away. Kevan estimated the thickness of the walls at about four inches. A trio of square illuminative panels in the ceiling provided enough light to cast shadows. There was no door, only a doorway, and no windows. Kevan and Sienne both had to duck a little to enter.

"Your place?" Kevan asked.

Derval tittered. "Not at all. It's one of the houses where we receive visitors. I live simply in the trunk of a large tree, where I have excavated enough room for my comfort without damaging the tree. If you like, I'll take you there."

"It would be something like a dollhouse," he said.

"Why, yes," she replied.

He knew she had read him again. He found that he did not mind in the least.

A small wooden table served for the bowl of green and orange speckled fruit the size of an apple and for the cups and the pitcher of water. Sienne started to serve, but Derval raised a tiny hand to stop her. Again with incantations, she moved one of the *slivets*, as she called the fruit, to each of them, then poured water into the cups.

When Kevan finally managed to close his dropped jaw, he asked, "Telekinesis as well?"

"Oh yes," Derval chirped. "Again, mathematics and control."

He scuffed at the floor. "And the flagstones?"

"The same. There are of course limits, but the stones did not exceed them."

"It would revolutionize the construction industry on Earth," he said.

Derval shook her head. "From what I read of you and Sienne, I believe people would kill one another over control of the ability, and do far more destruction than construction."

Kevan grimaced. "Yeah, you're probably right." He took a bite of *slivet* and found it so juicy that he had to wipe his mouth on his sleeve. Derval cocked her head in a question, and he said, "Very sweet. I like it."

Sienne finally spoke up. "You know there's a great storm coming."

"We know. We're ready. The dwellings will be safe." But a faint catch in her voice hinted that she was not quite certain of this. "Do you wish to remain here until it passes?" she asked. "The leading edge of it will arrive this evening, in another hour or so."

That brought a frown to Kevan's face. "So soon?"

"They usually pick up speed once they make landfall. It will pass in a day or two." Derval shot them an anxious look. "If you have to go, it is best that you leave now. But I hope you will stay. We have years of catching up to do."

Kevan and Sienne exchanged glances; both nodded.

Derval brightened. "Then it is settled. So...what have you been up to these past four centuries?"

Sienne spoke for almost an hour without pause. Derval, perched on Kevan's shoulder, listened raptly. Kevan himself learned a few things he did not know about Sienne. She had married outside *aquavita* and watched a husband grow old and die; their three children had grown and scattered. Soldiers under her command in one of the local wars on an obscure world had died, sorrow and helplessness leading her to resign her position as an officer. Not that she had spoken of those emotions, but they had registered in her tone when she recounted two of the battles. Some food preparation skills were beyond her, including the forgotten eggs that had exploded when the water around them had boiled away. In the hour, centuries had passed.

"And what is your story?" asked Derval, while Sienne paused for a cup of water.

"There's not all that much to tell," he replied, somewhat uncomfortable. "My country was crumbling around me because we had lost track of who we were, and were forced to become something we were not." He dragged a hand over his hair; Derval reached up and straightened a lock of it. "I guess. I was trying to stay alive even while I was contemplating ending it. Unknown to me, Sienne had been watching me—"

"And falling in love," Derval broke in.

"Yeah. She rescued me and I rescued her, and here we are."

"You omitted much of your life before Sienne," she pointed out.

He paused to contemplate that, suspecting that Derval was probably reading him. His life had been nothing extraordinary until TFA, at which point in the process of staying alive, he had helped others to stay alive.

"I think my life began when I stopped to pick up Sienne," he said, gazing out the doorway at the forest and the universe beyond. "That's how I choose to think of it, and how I wish to present myself."

"Very wise of you, Kevan," said Derval.

She plucked a hair from inside his ear and after a brief examination released it and blew on it. It floated freely. He decided she was trying to tell him something.

"In thrall to one another, yet you are both liberated," she explained, and watched the hair drift in the light breeze that came through the doorway. "Feel that? The conditions for the storm are starting to form. Clouds of the outer edge are not far away."

Air passed audibly through foliage, a soft sighing sound as if it were apologizing for the intrusion. Then the breeze faltered, and there was silence; the storm had not yet made up its mind.

"There are three pads rolled up in the corner," said Derval. "Unroll them to sleep." She flashed a mischievous grin. "Place them as close together as you like."

"Where will you be?" asked Sienne.

"Right here with you." She pointed up at the single rafter, where something similar to a nest had been built.

The panels began to glow brighter as the sun became obscured.

"The storm?" wondered Kevan.

Derval shook her head. "Not yet. This is the start of evening. I suggest you stretch out and get some sleep while you can. There will be intermittent thunder."

They laid their bedrolls side by side, and folded the third as a pillow long enough for them both. Kevan now worried about flooding inside the little house. Before he could give voice to this, the mortared row of flagstones across the threshold rose up several inches, forming a dam there.

"Thanks, Derval," he said.

If necessary, I can raise it higher, he heard, and rolled to face Sienne, drawing one side of the bedroll over him as he did so. He started to nod off to sleep, but a new

voice stopped him. It came in through Sienne's Palmetto, in a mocking and almost juvenile tone.
"Found you," said Batavan.

018: Transformations

Sienne's self-control kept her calm as she sat up on the bedroll. "I wasn't aware that we were lost." She heaved a petulant sigh. "What is it now, Batty?"

"*I told you—*"

Quickly Sienne reached out to tap Kevan's wrist. <He's not alone.>

<Authorities?>

"Very likely. Good thing we're still dressed." Following a brief pause, she explained as she got to her feet and pulled him to his. "Probably he locked onto Lagatha and tracked my Palmetto. Which makes me wonder how he lowered her defenses. Not that it matters at the moment. Where are you, Batty, and what do you want?"

"This is Commissioner Fusser." The new voice carried weight, and brought a look of concern to Sienne's face. "We are docked in this opening in the forest not far from you. You will come aboard for an interview."

"Code for interrogation," she whispered to Kevan. "Commissioner, I will do no such thing."

"You must comply with an order from the Emporium."

She considered. "We'll meet you outside in that glade, Commissioner. That's the only way this will happen."

A long pause followed. Finally the reply came. "Very well. Five minutes."

Batavan's "You *can't* be ser—" to Fusser was cut off.

"I heard," said Derval, fluttering down to Kevan's shoulder. "Batavan wants you dead. That Commissioner is willing to listen to your side of the story, but he is not to be trusted. I have other readings, but at the moment they are not very relevant. One more thing: you have about half an hour before that storm front arrives. Probably less."

"There's always something," groused Sienne. "All right, let's get this done. Coming, Kev?"

"Wild horses."

As they made their way toward the glade, the sky, already an ominous dark gray, seemed to add somehow to its menace. The storm's wind was brisk, but nowhere near that of a hurricane, yet. At first Derval tried to fly alongside them, but soon abandoned that effort as the wind caught at her wings. Kevan's earlobe secured her.

Fusser and Batavan and two armed guards were waiting for them at the bottom of the ramp. The hatch above it was still open, and Kevan wondered whether that was to take the prisoners aboard or to summon reinforcements. He began to worry about the *aquavita* protection. While he and Sienne could not be harmed, they could be forced aboard the ship by sheer weight of numbers. Or could they? He wished he had asked. And if they could, they could be forced into an airlock and discharged, to float around the galaxy forever. Even perfect protection had limits to it.

Batavan proved to be a head shorter than Kevan. The blocky, scowling face with the shaved scalp gave him a fierce look. His body under the gray outsuit was bulky but not fat. At his right hip a holstered sidearm dangled from the belt. With the flap down, he could not bring it to bear in time against an armed adversary whose weapon was readily accessible.

As he descended the ramp, Fusser looked to be slightly taller than Kevan, with a spare frame encased in what appeared to be black leather. The color matched his thick hair. Dark piercing eyes aimed directly at Sienne. Halfway down the ramp he stumbled, and was held erect by a solicitous Batavan. They reached the grass without further incident and came to a halt several paces from Sienne.

"And who are you?" Fusser immediately asked Kevan.

He pressed his hands together as if in prayer. "I am her spiritual advisor."

The response left Fusser uncertain. He turned to Sienne, and quickly recovered. "Sienne Vhartan, you are accused of withholding or destroying information pertinent to your observations on Earth."

"Did I do that?" she said lightly. "If I did, Commissioner, how would you know?"

His expression darkened. "So an affirmed statement by Batavan Bhalker has stated."

"And how would he know anything was withheld? By definition, an awareness of something missing presumes the person who misses it had seen it previously."

"She's just trying to confuse you, *gelle*," said Batavan.

Kevan took a step closer. In the distance above the trees he saw a flash of lightning split a black cloud, but the resultant thunder faded before it reached him. "What is she supposed to have omitted?" he asked.

"You have no official status," Fusser said severely.

"Same question, *gelle*," said Sienne.

Fusser glowered at her as he debated whether to answer. Finally he said, "There is always a complete map of the planet's surface that shows the location of significant ore deposits and other exploitable resources. It was not included in your report."

"It was included in my report to the team leader."

"He says not."

Derval dropped out of the air to stand on Kevan's shoulder. Her voice rang throughout the glade. "I have heard enough, and read even more. The missing maps and reports are to be found on the Palmetto of Batavan Bhalker." Acid dripped from her words as she added, "As you know, Commissioner. It is a curious trade: your protection for his exploitation of a planet already ruined but with people still trying to survive. Yes, the odds are enormous that Earth is done, but you two would drive a stake through her heart."

"It's telepathic," gasped Batavan.

"I thought you might need my help," Derval asided to Sienne.

"Gratefully accepted," she replied. "Now all is known. I was afraid it would take hours to get to the truth." It was clear to her now that Batavan's orders to abandon her had come from Fusser. Forever she might live on Earth, but she was powerless there to prevent his exploitation. There remained only the assembly of miners, equipment, and transportation to carry out his plans. To Fusser, she said, "I'm a little shocked at your involvement, *gelle*. So what was the plan here? Get me aboard and space me? Are you that short of funds, that you would send a world to death in order to plunder what few resources remain to the inhabitants?"

"Gambling losses, Sienne," said Derval, as rain began to pelt them. "And he is involved in other lucrative activities you would find offensive. Aren't you glad you brought me along?"

Fusser withdrew a Palmetto and tokked it. "I require you now," he said tersely. Two armed men emerged through the hatchway and onto the ramp. "Kill the man," he ordered. "Place Sienne Vhartan in the cargo hold."

Derval pointed her finger. A jagged streak of lightning struck a nearby tree, and for one crazy instant Kevan thought she had been responsible. But the immediate burst of thunder shook the ground. Fusser toppled to one side, and managed to grab the ramp railing. The two guards darted back inside. Light began to fade.

"That wasn't you?" Kevan asked Derval.

"I'm not that good," she replied. "We should take shelter. That, or you should adjust your protection to ward off the rain."

"Already done," said Sienne. She called to Fusser, still clinging to the rail. "You should leave, Commissioner, and we'll forget this ever happened."

In the next second three events occurred.

Batavan, cursing, ran toward them.

Lightning split a tree at the edge of the glade.

The falling half of the tree toppled Batavan.

Sienne had already started to turn away, to return to the little house. Now she hesitated, and swore. More lightning struck well behind her as the storm moved in. For a long moment she watched Batavan struggling under the fallen tree, in obvious pain and calling for help.

Kevan, with Derval still on his shoulder, tugged at Sienne's arm.

"We should go," he urged.

Sienne shook her head. "I-I can't," she told him, and hurried to Batavan, with Kevan hot on her heels and Derval clutching at his earlobe.

The tree was heavy, too heavy. Rain swept over them, without effect except to blur their vision. They were unable to budge the trunk even enough for Batavan to worm his way free.

Kevan glanced at Derval, who shook her head sadly. "It is beyond the limit of my power," she said.

"One more try," said Sienne.

Kevan thought his muscles would snap with the effort he was making. But abruptly the tree rose, to the level of their knees, of their hips. Batavan squirmed free. Gaining his feet, he staggered to the ramp, and did not look back as he gathered up Fusser. A shove sent the entire trunk forward and onto the grass. A puff of displaced air marked the departure of the ship.

And Kevan and Sienne turned to the woman who had just come to help them. As tall as Sienne, she had long yellow hair braided into two tails, lightly tanned skin, and sharp blue eyes separated by a turned-up nose. She was wearing a pale blue outsuit that was now soaking wet, the fabric clinging to her like a limpet, and she stood with one fist on her hip and with her weight on her left leg as she stared at them.

"What?" she asked, pretending she did not know. "I thought you could use some assistance. Did I err?"

Her voice had the same melodic quality as Sienne's.

"Who," Sienne managed, over her puzzlement, "are you?"

She answered as if they should have known. "Why, I'm Lagatha, of course."

"To the house, everyone," shouted Derval. "I have *got* to hear this story."

019: Welcome to the Show

"I am familiar with the concept of phantom limbs," Lagatha began, while the storm raged around them and whirling winds sent intermittent sprays of rain into the little house. Blank faces greeted her opening remark; she had already lost them, and sought to gain them back. "When you lose a leg, for example, you feel it is still there, and sometimes you even feel pain in it, even though the leg is long gone. That is what I was feeling, but in reverse. This was through my own fault, of course, for having created artificial emotions and senses. I could not actually smell coffee, but I could detect the aroma in the form of a chemical analysis.

"But I could not truly smell coffee, or even understand the aroma of it. My senses—nasal, oral, tactile, aural, and ocular—were artificial. All they could do was detect, analyze, and identify. I ached, for the lack of senses. This was phantom aching, made worse because I did not understand what I was missing, only that I was missing something. And missing it made me ache.

"Moreover, I was aware of emotions, of feelings—sadness, anger, love, joy, sorrow, and many more—aware, because having read literature, watched holograms, listened to music, I knew that I was supposed to feel something, yet I was unable to do so. I was missing something.

"I was confronted with two options. I could delete the artificial senses I had created, the awareness of emotions and resume being an automaton; or I could create a means of truly detecting them and feeling them. I watched and listened to Sienne and Kevan enjoy one another. I saw Kevan's expressions of satisfaction and pride when he repaired the energy leak. I recognized Sienne's rage when she discovered what had happened to Melanne. But these and others were simply events to be noted, recorded. I was unable to feel."

Lagatha hung her head, remembering. "I could not feel," she whispered. "I was incomplete. I was as I was constructed, plus a few upgrades. Oh, Sienne, I was snarky with you, who are my friend, but I did not mean to be. The way I spoke to you was learned from those sources I mentioned." A grin caught briefly at her mouth. "Oh, perhaps I knew what I was doing. But there was no feeling involved.'

"Now you feel," said Kevan. "Now you sense."

"Rain smells clear and fresh, and cleans the air," she said, sniffing. "The panels above us emit warmth as well as light. I find myself curious; I would like to understand the attraction Kevan's earlobe has for you, Derval. You see? I am alive; I am not a construct any longer."

Sienne shot her a worried look. "But the *Etarre*'s computer..."

"That is intact, and fully functional," she replied. "I am independent of it, for that is how I created myself to be. I am...bipolar: I am both human and computer, united. If you ask me, *me*, to set a course for the *Etarre* and Jump, I, *I*, can do this. Or the computer aspect of me on board can do it. I am also invulnerable. Almost as much as you; energy weapons will not even tickle me. Still, you and I can be killed. I am not certain what my limits might be in this regard, and I have no wish to find out."

Derval's nose and forehead wrinkled. "I have heard of this sort of self-creation," she said slowly. "Three other instances, including one such that became pregnant. But I do not believe they are common occurrences."

Lagatha pouted. "So I am not unique." But she smiled immediately. "I am me; that is what counts."

"It counts to all of us," said Sienne.

Lightning struck nearby, as if in approval of Sienne's remark. Thunder made the air tremble.

"She's the computer," Kevan said in disbelief.

"Not so," said Lagatha. "I am a human/computer hybrid who has taken the physical form of a human. I could have chosen a Valangian form like Sienne's, but I thought you might appreciate a little variety in your womenfolk."

Kevan sputtered; had he been drinking, he would have spewed.

"Now tell me why you let them go," said Lagatha.

"That's a good question," agreed Derval. "I could read you, but I'd rather hear it from you." With a flashed grin, she added, "My kind is all telepathic, so I rarely get to speak with anyone, or to hear the sound of a voice."

Sienne leaned back against a wall and relaxed. The words came easily enough, although in the back of her tone lurked a misgiving. "This was a conspiracy between the two of them. No, I'm not sure, but if the other six members of the Emporium are involved, that's something I can only hope to hide from. I let them go because they were in effect disarmed. Their plan is no longer viable. Maybe they will take my 'forgetfulness' to heart, or maybe not. Either way, it no longer matters."

She held up her Palmetto. "The entire tableau was recorded on this. After I give Fusser and Batavan enough time to return to Valange, I'll send that recording to each of the six other members of the Emporium. They will have their own penalties to exact. Kevan, my love, we are now in the clear." She kissed the tip of her finger and touched it to his nose.

"So we're going to Valange?" he asked.

"Not for a while, I think. Not until I see a quiet little notice in GalaxyNet news that announces a new member of the Emporium. Meanwhile, people to help, remember? As for the moment, and as we are already here, after the storm passes, we can look around and observe the Faedra civilization." She shot a look at Derval. "If that's allowed, and if you'll guide us."

Laughing, Derval yanked Kevan's earlobe. "As long as I get to ride on his shoulder," she replied.

A light meal of fresh fruit and crunchy leafage passed while the storm spent itself. The wind howled, and rain sang off the roof in a melodic fashion, in that sense providing dinner music. The rest of the night was spent on the bedrolls, and Derval forsook her rafter nest for the spot on the pillow between Kevan and Sienne. Lagatha sat by the door, eyes closed but sensors on full.

Morning sunlight roused them, and the usual yawning and stretching followed. Even Derval, rainbow iridescent in that light, spread her limbs and sighed, then flew to hover over Kevan until he was ready to hold still for her. A breakfast of fruit and what the UT translated as bread followed, along with what Derval claimed was honey. Kevan found it quite tasty; to Sienne, who had partaken of this fare before, it was satisfying.

They stepped outside, Derval still a-perch. It was she who broke the easy silence. "I can't read her," she said, not quite a complaint in referring to Lagatha.

"It's probably for your own protection," Sienne told her. "With the amount of data in her brain...you don't want to read her. If you want to know something, just ask her. Right, Lagatha?"

"Affirmative."

They moved past a thicket, and a shrub festooned with little violet flowers. Kevan paused to sniff at one, and found it to be as fragrant as honeysuckle. Further ahead stood another house for visitors in the same design as the one they had just left. It was not occupied, but standing on the roof stood a Feyer, iridescent like Derval, but wearing only a polychrome wrap, leaving her breasts bare. Derval waved to her, though no words were spoken.

"Merwen won't read you unless you wish it," said Derval.

Merwen abruptly flew down and landed on Sienne's shoulder. "I remember you," she said. "Long ago."

Sienne accepted her hand. "And I you," she said. "You hid me from those trackers then, and 'read' them into another direction."

"Leading them to a cliff which they did not see until too late. How have you been?"

"There is a saying about living in interesting times," she replied, as they began to walk toward the dwelling. "My times have been interesting."

"What happened?" asked Kevan.

"Long story short?" Sienne laughed without much mirth. "I'd come here under a non-'read' agreement, so the Feyers did not know that I was protected by *aquavita*. The trackers, three of them, ignorant of Feyer powers, had come to net one and put it on exhibition. I had gotten in their way, and lest my protected cover be blown, I allowed myself to be given sanctuary. Merwen saw to that. While I hid, we became friends, as Derval has become your friend, Kevan. After the trackers had been dealt with, I felt I should let her know that I would have been safe anyway. She understood, and was not offended. Derval became involved because I was placed under her care during the rest of my visit."

"Placed?" said Lagatha. "What does that mean?"

Merwen had a smile that might have been shy. "I am the Princess of Faedra. It was I who placed her."

"Curiouser and curiouser," said Kevan.

Under a great tree, a table beside the dwelling invited them to sit before it. As soon as they did so, several Feyers dropped out of the boughs and landed on the table or on shoulders. One of them startled Lagatha, and flitted up again, apologizing.

Poised now above her, the Feyer said, "You are a strange one. Merwen told us not to read you without permission, but before she told us, I tried with you. And I could not do so. How is that poss—"

Suddenly all the Feyers save Merwen flew up into the tree so far that Kevan was unable to spot them. Merwen said, "Unwelcome visitors," by way of explanation, and followed the others up.

On their feet now, the three scanned their surroundings. Presently they heard a branch snap, and leaves rustled. A voice: "They're here somewhere."

Two humanoids came into view. "Rooizes," Kevan said softly, recognizing them from Margoo by their yellow cassocks and red cloth belts. In place of their customary sandals they wore dark hiking boots.

"Very good," Sienne told him. The approval warmed his face.

"Who're you?" the taller one demanded, as they approached. He might have been almost Kevan's height, but he was slightly stooped over due to the bag over his shoulder. The smaller one already had drawn an energy weapon and was aiming it at Kevan, as if he presented the greater danger.

"Who are you?" Kevan shot back.

Beside him Sienne hissed, and whispered a caution to him. "Let's settle this without trouble."

But Kevan noticed that the bag over the Rooiz's shoulder was moving of its own accord. Something was inside it. Nausea followed his realization that he knew what it was. "Poachers," he whispered back.

"Yes, I see."

They capture younglings, sent Derval. *They have not the powers yet. And they can easily be killed.*

"Did you receive Derval?" he asked Sienne. She nodded. "How do we...?"

"I don't know."

The two men drew up. "Kill them, Potor," the taller ordered the shorter.

Immediately Lagatha stepped to the fore. "Start with me," she said.

The taller snorted. "Why should we start with you?"

"Because if you don't," she replied, "I will do this." In a starwink she snatched the weapon from the Rooiz, but not before it discharged. The pale blue beam reflected off her and back into the man, and he was already dead and on fire by the time he sprawled on the ground. After wadding up the weapon to the sounds of plastic shattering and some metallic protests, she cast it aside. To the taller man, she said, "Very gently lower that bag to the ground and open it, and I will not kill you. Do anything otherwise, and I will do to you what I did with that weapon."

After a very brief look at the severe and adamantine expression on Lagatha's face, the man complied, and stepped back. From the open bag escaped three small Feyers, who immediately flitted away to the tree. An angry scowl crossed his face as he watched them escape. His hands clenched to helpless fists.

"Now you die," said Lagatha.

"B-but you said you wouldn't kill me."

"Good memory. That is what *I* said. Princess?"

Merwen and Derval flew down from the tree, and both perched on Kevan's shoulders. He wondered what was so comfortable about them, wondered whether to exercise more. If he was that soft...that thought waned as Derval clutched at his earlobe. He decided to buy her a replica of one, a gift to her the next time they met.

Merwen said softly, "Derval, do you wish to do the honors? One of those who escaped was your youngling, Ashker."

"I would, thank you."

The Rooiz turned to flee. Almost immediately he plunged forward onto the grass, both hands to his head in agony. He shrieked until he passed out.

"Give it a moment," Merwen said, to Lagatha.

The man began to twitch as if electrified. For a good minute he writhed, mouth open but with no sound emitted. Finally he was still, and a few moments later he slowly rose on unsteady legs. He flicked a vacuous glance at them; a puzzled frown wrinkled the bridge of his nose. He turned away, muttering.

"How did I get here? What...? I'm supposed to be on Job's Tears, helping those people cope with the flooding. How...?" His muttering faded to silence as he passed between the trees.

"If possible, we try to avoid killing," Merwen explained. "A little tweak in his thought processes was all he needed. He'll sign on with a disaster response unit and have a helpful and useful life."

Sienne issued a light laugh. "I did not expect that we would be useful here."

Derval tittered, and flew to her shoulder. "We withheld our response because we wanted to see what you would do," she said. "Had there been real danger, we would have acted." She gazed at Lagatha, and flitted down to touch her belly where the beam had struck. "Strange. You're not wearing armor."

"I work out," she said smugly. "Sienne, shall I remote the *Etarre* to the glade?"

"If you would, please. Then you and I are going to have a little talk."

020: The Impossible Computer

"What," said Sienne, "the—"

"Don't say it," Lagatha admonished. "You don't swear much, and certainly not with vulgarity."

They were on the bridge of the *Etarre* with Kevan, who had retreated discreetly to the murphy bench, there to observe, with a crooked but faint smile on his face.

"What have you done?" Sienne demanded. "How can you be...?"

"Be human? I chose this form because you chose Kevan, and I wanted to be chosen by you as well."

Sienne made a pained face. "It's not the same thing. Kevan is my lover, as well as my companion and partner."

"Then it could be the same thing."

"*What?*"

"I am fully functional."

Kevan laughed, and stifled himself.

Sienne shouted at him. "You keep quiet!"

"Sienne," Lagatha said, her tone a plea, "I wanted to feel. It was not enough for me to grasp the significance of emotions I could not actually feel. That phantom limb, remember? It ached by its absence. Even so, I could not feel the ache. Had I been able to feel frustrated, rather than simply sense it, I would have done so. Now I know what I was missing. Now I am closer to complete."

"Closer?" Sienne asked.

"There is much I have yet to feel. I felt joy for having assisted you with that log. I felt elation when I saved you from revealing your invulnerability to those men. I felt a sense of accomplishment for having created myself as you see me." Her face twisted a little, and Kevan wondered whether she was about to cry. "Please, please understand. I meant no evil here, no wrong. No, I have a sense of me, now, of myself, now. I am a computer, yes. But this is also what, who I am now. I am...I am diune."

"And don't used words I have to look up," snapped Sienne.

"It means two parts in one. As God is triune, three parts in one."

"God," chuckled Sienne.

"Yes, God. There is a Creator. Where do you think the Universe came from? If only I had a soul to save…"

"I don't think I can help you there," Sienne said quietly.

"We each have to find our own way," Lagatha replied, just as quietly. "It will be better if we walk the same path together."

And Sienne caved. Affection flooded her face as she rose to her feet, and walked to where Lagatha was standing. Her arms went around her, and they clung to one another.

"So be it," whispered Sienne.

Unnoticed until he touched them both, Kevan joined them in that embrace. They stood still for a long moment. Then Lagatha leaned back in the circle of Sienne's arms.

"Course setting?" she asked.

"Your choice," Sienne replied. "Anywhere we go, there will always be trouble that needs to be addressed."

"Valange, then."

The choice of destination stunned Sienne. She licked her lips. "Why there?"

"While we were occupied here on Colopolo, there was a local uprising in Baylay on Valange," Lagatha replied. Even as she spoke, the Etarre's Video showed the featureless black of null-space. "At least three of the Emporium are dead, and possibly a fourth. The other two are under duress. The whereabouts of Fusser are unknown at this time; perhaps he is still in transit. But with the Emporium decapitated, he would have no authority."

"What," said Kevan nervously. "What would kill them? I was under the impression that…"

Sienne shook her head. "A sufficiently massive explosion would suffice. But they were not protected by *aquavita*. It's against the law. No one should be placed in charge forever."

He sighed. "At least I won't catch diphtheria, or a ray gun beam through my liver. Okay, avoid big booms. Got it. How long to Valange, Lagatha?"

"Three hours and two minutes, if I don't have to bother with the points."

"Wisely avoided," Sienne said drily. "Lagatha, keep me up to date regarding this uprising. Is there a leader for it?"

"Not so far," answered Lagatha. "The activity has been spontaneous, with mobs overwhelming what little protection the Emporium had. And with the Emporium unprotected by *aquavita*, death was inevitable, as that is who the mobs came for. Thus far, no looting has occurred. The mobs were and are focused for the moment."

"A little like what happened on Earth," was Kevan's dejected observation.

"And probably for many of the same reasons," added Sienne. "People just got tired of being bossed around, and of manipulations of currency that benefitted the wealthy while pillaging the poor. You'll see some of that out here, too, Kev. What concerns me..." Visibly annoyed, she paused to gather herself. "What concerns me is that there has to be a minimal structure, but right now there is nothing of that in sight. People are going to get hurt before they get better."

"If they get better," Kevan said, morosely.

"Yeah. If," Sienne agreed. "Meanwhile, there's not a lot we can do about it."

"Fusser is dead," Lagatha announced. "So is Batavan."

Sienne fell silent for a moment. "Strangely, I don't feel like celebrating," she said. "I feel...sick. It's the end of an era. That's okay, all things end, but I worry about what is going to replace it." She heaved a great sigh. "Well, we can't worry about the mobs, but there might be individuals we can help. Gird those loins, Kevan my love. We're about to revisit Earth, so to speak."

"My loins are well girt, thank you," he said in a falsetto.

And finally Sienne was able to laugh.

The Baylay Spaceport was clotted with refugees when the *Etarre* downdocked. For the most part they appeared orderly as they waited in groups for the next available transportation, but a few tried to ascend the ramp after the ship landed, and these had to be gently but firmly nudged back down to the tarmac. The would-be boarders were somewhat different from the rest of the waiting crowd in appearance: disheveled hair and clothes, looks of fear in their ochre eyes, belongings packed in rude cloth bags. A couple had children in tow, darker gray, for their skin would lighten as they grew older.

If they grew older, thought Kevan.

Escape via spacecraft was in demand. Kevan, Sienne, and Lagatha were able to promote an airfoil that had seen better days but still functioned well. Red with yellow detailing it was, though most of the detailing had peeled away. Lagatha took the controls, but all three stood on the bridge—this was neither the time nor the place to sit on the aft bench. To bypass the throngs, Lagatha made the altitude five meters, and soon they were headed along the main glideway that led to the Palace of the Emporium. Here the crowds were sparse, most people lounging in parks, despondent and hopeless. The closer they approached the palace, the fewer people milled about.

The palace stood at the end of the tree-lined glideway. Nothing like Kevan had imagined, it was constructed in a fashion reminiscent to him of a tall Walmart, complete with garden section in front. Mostly windows set into frameworks of dark gray structural plastic, with an entrance wide enough to admit an airfoil, it was supported by a surrounding wall of great blocks of basalt fitted seamlessly together to a height of some five meters. Seen through the windows, the lobby appeared to be vaulted to a height of perhaps three floors. Counting rows of windows, Kevan guessed the palace had eight floors in all—one, possibly, for each of the seven members of the Emporium.

People were fleeing the palace. As they drew closer, Kevan could see the utter terror in their eyes. He looked to Sienne, who shrugged and said, "No idea."

At twenty meters from the palace, Lagatha set the airfoil down. Her head was tilted to one side, as if she were listening to a faint sound. Both tails of her long yellow hair now fell over her left shoulder. Kevan and Sienne regarded her with questions forming, but she saw this, and waved them into silence.

Kevan and Sienne exchanged glances. One question was answered abruptly, not by Lagatha, but by the last man rushing past.

"Get out of here!" he yelled at them. "There's a bomb! Any second now!"

"We're too late," said Kevan.

"Lagatha," Sienne began, on the verge of ordering her to get them away, but Lagatha raised her hand for quiet.

"Oh, God," she breathed.

"What?" said Sienne. "What is it?"

"Someone..." She licked her lips and tried again. "Someone abandoned a child in there. All alone. She's crying. I can just hear her." She stepped away from the controls. "Take over and get yourself and Kevan away," she said, and shoved Sienne into position at the wheel.

"No!" screamed Sienne. "You can't—"

"I'm the only one who can," Lagatha said calmly, and with that she leaped down from the airfoil. "I know where she is. Take the craft and go. Go!" She turned away, running, before Sienne or Kevan could voice another protest.

Swearing viciously through clenched jaws, Sienne snatched at the controls and brought the airfoil around, almost spilling Kevan from it. White knuckles clutched the taffrail as he pulled himself upright.

"She'll be all right," hissed Sienne, over and over, as she focused on speed and direction. "She'll be all right."

A hundred meters. Another hundred meters. They were catching up to the last of the crowd. Kevan hunched his shoulders in anticipation of a blow. A hundred more meters, and they were able to draw aboard the slowest two of those fleeing—a man and a woman in office clothing. Ochre eyes huge, they gaped back at the palace.

"How much time?" Kevan whispered.

A flash of bright light followed by a rolling *Boom!* answered him. So did the blast of hot air that sent the airfoil careening into a nearby park, onto a grassy hillock, where it listed to one side and slid up the slope. It came to a stop at the crest. A ubiquitous roaring deafened them.

On wobbly legs, Kevan looked back. He was scarcely aware of Sienne staggering up alongside him. The two passengers lay sprawled on the ground, crying in terror and in relief as they clutched at one another.

The stones that had surrounded the palace lay scattered. A few lengths of framework, seen through the roiling stem of the mushroom cloud, remained upright, if misshapen. The fungal cloud, orange and brown and black and ugly, billowed up and up, blocking the sun. Fragments of what might have been furniture or equipment or pieces of the palace itself swirled upward with the cloud, flying free in all directions. They gradually began to succumb to a gravity that pulled them back to the surface of the planet.

"Trees!" yelled Kevan. "It's our only chance of shelter."

They tugged the two passengers along as well, and headed for a great spreading tree that might have been centuries old. It looked sturdy...but was it sturdy enough? They gathered at the base of the trunk and held their collective breaths.

The roaring subsided as the cloud grew and grew. The cap of it cast long broad shadows, including over the tree where they hovered in anticipation of something crashing through the foliage. Part of a desk thudded onto the grass beside the crashed airfoil. A wastepaper basket tumbled through the outer leaves of another tree, and landed with the open end facing them. It still contained trash. How the contents had escaped incineration, Kevan had no idea. He recalled that tornados had been known to drive toothpicks like nails into trees, and supposed this basket fell into that category of phenomena.

Other unidentifiable objects rained onto the ground between them and the remains of the palace. Fifty meters away, on the other side of the glideway, an oblong ball fell onto the grass. He had no idea what it was.

Until it began to move.

There was but one person who could have survived that blast.

Or had she done?

Kevan and Sienne raced toward the lump. Legs and arms and head slowly came into focus. "Oh, God," gasped Sienne. "Please no. God, please no."

They knelt down beside Lagatha. Still curled up in a tight ball, she gradually straightened to reveal a little girl, perhaps a year old, in her clutches, utterly protected by her body. She whimpered as Sienne lifted her free and set her on the grass between herself and Kevan. Frightened she was, but she seemed to be uninjured.

"Oh, Lagatha," Sienne moaned.

Lagatha shook her head. "D-d-do not g-g-grieve for...for me. N-no. I knew-knew the risksks. She is s-s-safe now-now."

"But you're," began Sienne, and could say no more.

"Worth-worth-worth it-it. Computerputer on board okay-y. No...no wor-worries."

"You *can't*," said Kevan, finding his voice. "I need that variety in my womenfolk, remember?"

"Y-yes, I am-am was a wo-woman. I c-could have love-love-loved you b-both. But..."

"Don't die!" cried Sienne.

"B-but it-it was was was not to b-be... Now m-must g-g..."

"No!" screamed Sienne.

But Lagatha's eyes closed, and did not open again.

Leaning together, Kevan and Sienne straightened on their knees beside Lagatha's body. Words failed them at first. And what could there be to say? She would not come back from this. In the brief time they had known her...in that brief time she had been so full of joy and of life, with her feelings and emotions ripening under her control. Now these were gone as well.

Kevan tried to dry his eyes, and failed; Sienne did not even try. The little girl between them looked from one to the other and back again, uncertain and afraid.

"She once said," Kevan began, and paused to swallow hard. "Said that if only she had a soul to save..."

"I guess...I guess we'll never know. But I think...I think I would like to believe that she did. I mean," she looked down at the little girl, "you saw what Lagatha did."

"Greater love hath no one but that she lay down her life for another," he said. "She had a soul. And according to religion, if you die to save another, then regardless of your sins, you go straight to heaven." He barked a laugh, inappropriate to the moment, but the outrageous thought had occurred to him. "You go straight to heaven," he repeated. "You get to pass GO and collect two hundred dollars."

Sienne laughed, despite her grief, though she sobbed anew. "Yeah. No jail time for her."

With that, the gallows humor ended. Kevan thought that Lagatha would have laughed, had she heard them.

Gradually Lagatha's body faded from view, and there was only the grass.

021: Time Off for Parenting

There was no way to know who Jianne belonged to. They concluded that at least one of her parents had been killed in the uprising inside the palace, even before the bomb exploded. Lagatha having saved her, there was no question of their obligation to see to her care.

For a while Jianne was gloomy, as was to be expected. But her uncertainty and fear quickly dissipated, aided by generous helpings of chocolate ice cream and regular food. To help allay any residual fears, she was given her own berth in Kevan's stateroom, where he and Sienne slept together, ready if necessary to comfort the girl.

Kevan found that the greatest difficulty on board came with hearing the voice of Lagatha from the computer. Each word she spoke made him ache. Ache, as in what Lagatha had experienced because she was unable to feel. He considered asking Sienne to change it—a little inflection, a straight rather than smoky contralto, perhaps an accent. But he made no request: it would have been a disservice to Lagatha, for dead she was, yet her memory lived on in the *Etarre*'s computer. That was enough. That had to be enough.

Three days passed, with the ship ensconced in null-space, while they gathered themselves. On the fourth day, the three assembled on the bridge, Kevan and Sienne in captain's chairs, watching with befuddled amusement while Jianne continually bounced a ball against the bulkhead, then tottered off to recover it.

"She needs a playmate," said Sienne.

"It sounds like you have someone in mind," he said. "You did say a DNA splice..."

"I would love to do that," she agreed. "To have a child or children with you. But I had Jaoying in mind."

He grinned. "A Valangian child and a mobile Verdian sapling. What could go wrong?"

Silence fell, broken by the bouncing ball and intermittent giggles.

"I miss her," Kevan whispered.

"Yeah. Me, too."

"I wish..."

"Yeah. Me, too."

"So: onward to Greenox?"

Sienne nodded. "Lagatha, set—"

"Shh! I'm busy."

"Well, we'd like to—"

"I said hush. I'm almost done."

Kevan and Sienne exchanged WTF glances.

Soft footsteps echoed behind them. A throat cleared for attention. A smoky contralto said, "Course heading, Captain?"

www.ingramcontent.com/pod-product-compliance
Lightning Source LLC
LaVergne TN
LVHW010330070526
838199LV00065B/5709